PACIFIC
INTRIGUE

ALLAN CARSON

Printed in Canada

For information address:
Durban House Publishing Company, Inc.
7502 Greenville Avenue, Suite 500, Dallas, Texas 75231
214.890.4050

Library of Congress Cataloging-in-Publication Data
Allan Carson, 1928

Pacific Intrigue / by Allan Carson

Library of Congress Catalog Card Number: 00-2002115649

p. cm.

ISBN 1-930754-31-0

First Edition

10 9 8 7 6 5 4 3 2 1

Visit our Web site at
http://www.durbanhouse.com

Book design by:
Strasbourg-MOOF, GmBH

For my wife, Nancy

"There Will Never Be Another You"

Acknowledgements

Thank you to Richard Sand (novelist & my editor) and John Lewis (novelist & publisher)—! and to Diane Cook who led me to them.

Thanks to my wife, Nancy, for her astute proof-reading. Thanks also to her and to our friends for their encouragement.

PACIFIC
INTRIGUE

PROLOGUE

In the Seattle area known as the Gulch, two men from Fiji walked along the sidewalk of a side street where they shared a rented room. They were wearing stained trousers and T-shirts with sweaters that had seen better days. Neither wore socks on his sandaled feet. Each individual was dark faced in both complexion and expression.

The taller of the two had a scar on his left cheek. His name was Satala, and he had a reputation for fighting and petty crime. The second man, Rakai, was short and vicious.

They walked along, still stiff from their stowaway on a truck from Vancouver. Their destination was a brown frame house that was fronted by a picket fence. To the left side of the house was a detached garage.

Satala opened the gate, and they walked to the front door. He pressed the doorbell.

After a minute or so they heard footsteps inside.

"Yes? Who is there?"

"Friends from Fiji," said Satala.

The man opened the chained door a crack. "We do not know you."

"No, but we know you are Hassan and Harakh and we want to speak to you," continued Satala.

"Wait a minute." The door closed again and reopened, but there was no light inside.

"You may both enter, but keep your hands out in front of you."

Satala and Rakai moved forward. "Don't look around until you're told to do so."

They heard the sound of another person entering from the other side of the room.

"Who are you and what do you want?"

"We are from Fiji, and we work there with some of your colleagues," said Satala.

"What are your names?"

"I am called Satala and my friend's name is Rakai."

"What are the names of those that you worked with in Fiji?"

"The ones you know are Saliheen and Aziz."

There was a pause, and then the light was switched on in the room and the two Pakistani occupants showed themselves for the first time.

"Why did they send you here?" asked Hassan. "We were not informed that you would be coming."

"They did not send us. Coming here was our own idea."

Hassan gestured with his black pistol toward the dining table. "Both of you sit down, but keep your hands above the table."

The Fijians sat down at the dining table.

"And just what did you plan to do here, and what do you want to see us for?" asked the other Pakistani, Harakh.

"We want to be paid for our work in Fiji. We do not think that Saliheen and Aziz were fair to us in the amount they gave us."

Hassan laughed. "What makes you think that we'd pay you more than he did?"

"If you don't pay us what we are owed, then we will let the local police know what you're planning here."

"We can kill you both here and now," snarled Harakh.

"Let us not be hasty," said Hassan and then went on. "And how much do your Fijian friends think would be a fair amount for your services?"

"We want ten thousand American dollars."

Hassan laughed again. "Why should we pay you anything? I think we should just get rid of you both."

Rakai could keep his silence no longer. "Our friends in Fiji are waiting to hear from us, and if they don't, then they will inform the authorities of your plot."

Hassan gestured with his big pistol and glanced at Harakh. "Tie them up and gag them. We must deal with these fools before they give us any more trouble."

Hassan kept his pistol on the two Fijians as his partner tied and gagged them. The prisoners were blindfolded and led outside to the garage, where they were put in the back of a green Dodge sedan.

Hassan drove to a remote area in the hills. The two men were brought out of the car and made to sit on the ground. Hassan and Harakh, as if choreographed, approached their trembling victims from behind and slashed their throats.

ONE

Doctor Peter Barclay eased back the throttles on the *Noqui Tau*, his thirty-four foot cruiser. The roar of the diesels lessened to a gentle throbbing as he turned the wheel to bring the boat towards the entrance of the channel that led into Pacific Harbour.

Moving along the cut, they passed the old Pacific Harbour hotel, now called The Centra Resort, on the starboard side. There were several craft moored along the hotel bulkhead, including dive boats and fishing cruisers as well as a large boat used for taking hotel guests on snorkeling and picnic cruises. Behind the bulkhead the lawn extended past the tennis courts and up to the hotel buildings. To port was "The Pub," a restaurant and bar, set in a large old Fijian home.

Barclay's deckhand was Jone, a big Fijian. They had been out since dawn, and their four-hour trip had been rewarded with two fine wahoo that were now residing in the fish bin overlying the scupper on the port side. Jone lowered the antennae and began to stow some of the gear.

The cruiser continued along the canal, a man-made inlet from the sea, and passed under the bridge supporting the Queen's Highway. The main road went around the coast of Fiji's largest island, Viti Levu, and stretched from Lautoka to Suva. A little further along, remnants of the old unsealed gravel road that had stretched all the way across Viti Levu until the 1970's could still be seen.

Pacific Harbour is a residential community of many homes, here known as villas. The seventy-five hundred acres also encompass a Robert Trent Jones golf course. This was one more thing that added to Peter's enjoyment of the area where he lived. Also the price was right. He could not have all these things in Hawaii.

Peter Barclay, M.D., had been living in Fiji for the past two years, but had been holidaying there for over twenty. All the vacation trips were made with his wife, Julie. She had been his best friend as well as his lover. When she was killed in a car crash three years before, he did not know if he could survive.

He filled his life with his work as a pathologist in a Seattle hospital, but soon that was less than satisfying for him. The practice of medicine had changed with more regulations and less "real doctoring." Many of his friends in the profession had retired, and others wished to quit. Peter assessed his situation as he would a complex case. He gave three months notice and sold their home. Their other possessions were divided amongst Julie's favorite charities.

Strangely, the decision of where to live in retirement was not difficult. Fiji seemed to be a natural move for him. It had always been their place, his and Julie's together.

Winding along the waterway, the *Noqui Tau* finally came around a bend to approach the small float that was home to her. There was a ramp connecting the float to a deck on the lawn at the water's edge, the ramp now sloping gently as it was near to full tide. Behind the moorage was a four-bedroom villa with a high peaked roof.

On the other side of the house was a turquoise pool surrounded by a high growth of plants and flowers, including flamboyant trees, hibiscus and frangipani. There were also many fruit trees, with bananas, papaya and pineapple in abundance.

Ramesh, the gardener and otherwise handyman, stood waiting, having spotted the boat when she rounded the last bend in the waterway on her approach to the villa. He was one of the Indian population in Fiji whose predecessors had come to the islands in the nineteenth century. A large black dog was swaying back and forth, jumping and barking excitedly by Ramesh's side on the float. The dog was mostly black lab, and Peter had named him Koli, which in Fijian simply means "dog." Ramesh grabbed his collar to keep the animal from launching himself into the water to greet the *Noqui Tau* and her crew.

Peter brought the boat alongside, putting the engines in reverse briefly to slow her to a stop, and Ramesh handed the mooring line attached to the float to Jone, who looped it over the stern cleat. Then they both moved ahead and repeated the process at the bow. Ramesh secured a spring line to complete the procedure as Peter shut down the diesels.

"What's new, Ramesh? Have you been behaving yourself, you old scoundrel?" asked Peter, and the dark skinned man grinned with a flash of white teeth.

"Oh yes boss, as always," he replied.

"I'll bet," responded Peter as he climbed over the rail on to the float. "We've some wahoo for you to clean, and you can help Jone wash down the boat and stow the fishing gear."

He walked up the ramp from the float and continued along the path that curved upwards across the lawn and through the shrubbery. He removed his boat shoes and entered the house through the back door, leaving the dog outside.

Mere, his housegirl, was in the kitchen and turned as he entered.

"*Nisa yadra,* Mere, and how are you today?" Peter said.

"Good morning, Doctor. Did you have good fishing?"

"Two wahoo, which should make for very nice eating. I hope there's plenty of room in the freezer, but you get some to take home too."

He poured a glass of fresh orange juice, added some ice cubes and a liberal slug of Bounty overproof Fijian rum. He called it "OP-OJ"—"Overproof and orange juice."

Drink in hand, he headed for his bathroom on the master bedroom side of the house and turned on the shower. He stripped off his clothes and, after another swallow of the fortified fruit juice, luxuriated in the spray before soaping himself and rinsing off.

After toweling off and dressing in shorts and a T-shirt, Peter headed to his office on the other side of the villa. Then he went to the computer and turned it on. After it was booted up, he went on line and checked his incoming email.

Later he wished he hadn't.

TWO

Air Pacific flight 811 landed early at Nadi International Airport due to favorable winds and the absence of any nasty squalls to spoil the comfort of the passengers.

The multicolored B747-200 taxied from the end of the runway and approached its place at the terminal. Passengers began to arise before it had come to a complete stop and began opening the overhead bins. After crushing together in the aisles, they then got to stand there for some ten minutes before disembarkation actually began.

The passenger in 17C stayed in his seat, examining the other passengers carefully from years of habit on the Seattle P.D. Looking for trouble before it happened was the routine for Detective Gerry McCann.

Four rows behind was a dark man of Middle Eastern appearance. He talked easily with the passengers around him and left without a hint that he had been watching McCann throughout the flight.

Exiting the plane, McCann felt the warm, humid climate wrap around him. He stopped on the long ramp to remove his jacket and hang it over his arm as he walked with his fellow passengers towards the terminal entrance. The folks going on to Australia split off from the others to enter the transit lounge, where the duty free merchants were preparing to sell them all manner of goods, from liquor to stereo equipment, cameras, watches, clothing and books, as well as Fijian artifacts and handicrafts. Those disembarking in Fiji filed into the immigration hall to join one of several long lines, which moved very slowly towards the officials at the desks.

The dark man made it in line well ahead of McCann. He had a large carry-on suitcase and also a sizable briefcase, and in the customs area he showed no interest in the empty carousel but headed straight for the inspection desk. After a brief conversation with the inspector, he then proceeded through the door to the outer waiting area.

Turning to the right, he went outside to where the cars were parked. He continued along the row of vehicles, glancing at the license plate of each until he found the number he sought. Placing his bags on the sidewalk, he went to the right side of the tan colored Subaru and, opening the door, sat on the driver's seat. From under the seat he withdrew the car keys and then went to the rear, where he opened the trunk. Removing the cover from the spare wheel well, he inserted his hand and withdrew a package. He then placed the package under the front seat, locked the doors,and strolled back inside the terminal to mingle with the crowd.

McCann purchased a couple of bottles of Stolichnaya at the duty free store and then awaited the arrival of his one suitcase. Exiting the customs hall, he found a crowd outside, some being greeted, but many having the somewhat lost appearance that travelers assume when they arrive in a foreign land and don't quite know what to do next. He watched the many locals who were approaching the new arrivals and offering their services. Most represented hotels or were taxi drivers looking for a fare. One of them approached him.

"Detective McCann?" he said, and the cop nodded.

"I am Ram Nair, and I've been sent to meet you. Welcome to Fiji"

"Thank you," said McCann.

They walked along the line to a green Toyota station wagon. Nair opened the tailgate and placed the suitcase inside. The dark skinned man walked by and got into the Subaru parked a little further along the row of cars.

The Toyota pulled out and headed towards the airport exit. The Subaru followed and, after passing the gate, both cars turned right onto the main road, the Queen's Highway, in the direction of Nadi. Even at this late hour, there were quite a few cars on the road. The Subaru changed lanes and stayed well behind.

Crossing over the bridge, they drove through Nadi. The storefronts were shuttered and boarded up.

Beyond Nadi the traffic decreased and the Subaru fell back a bit, but keeping in sight of the Toyota's taillights. The driver of the following car reached under his seat, extracted the package, and placed it by his side on the other seat. With his left hand he unwrapped the paper and felt the hard outline of a Walther PPK. There was also a roll of bills and a box of ammunition.

The Toyota and then the Subaru passed several villages, and after about fifty minutes they entered the town of Sigatoka. This town also was deserted, and after crossing over the bridge in the town center, they continued east into the quiet countryside. They passed through several villages during the next hour and then the road turned inland through lush tropical hills for some miles before heading back towards the coast. McCann could see the white surf in the moonlight. He knew that they had reached his destination of Pacific Harbour when they crossed over a bridge with the Centra Resort on their right.

THREE

The Toyota followed the curving driveway to the front of the villa and became bathed in floodlights activated by a sensor over the front door.

The arrival was announced raucously by the large black dog as Dr. Peter Barclay came out to greet his guest.

When McCann stepped out and stretched his limbs, somewhat stiff from the long trip, the doctor stepped forward.

"Hello," he said, extending his hand to the detective. "I'm Peter Barclay. Welcome to Pacific Harbour."

"Gerry McCann," said the detective.

Ram Nair had already taken McCann's baggage out of the car, and Peter held the door open for McCann.

Peter went to the refrigerator and uncapped two bottles of Fiji bitter, known as "stubbies" because of their squat shape. He did not get out any glasses, following the local custom of drinking from the bottle, each placed in a Styrofoam container to keep it cool and also to limit condensation.

"Bula," toasted Peter. McCann nodded. They drank in silence.

"Okay. What's this all about?" Peter asked abruptly.

"I'm a Detective with the Seattle Police as a part of their anti-terror task force. I was working a case with ties to your exotic land here." The beer bottle waved around. "The Feds want to stay out of it right now. Otherwise they'd have to go through the State Department and all that, which can cause what they call 'an incident' and I call red tape bullshit. Anyway, I worked with Bill Childers, the M.E. He mentioned you're from Seattle, and I came up with the idea that I'm here as one of your old colleagues. Got me booked on the plane as 'Doctor.'"

"Pete—I guess everybody in Seattle calls you 'Pete'?" McCann paused, and the doctor nodded. "If I check into a hotel here by myself, I'll stand out like a boil on a baby's backside."

"Do I have a say in this?"

"Not really. You could get me another cold one, though."

Peter got up and uncapped another couple of beers.

"You're not convincing me that I shouldn't be asking you to get the hell out of here."

"Let me start by asking you, doctor, what you know about the Muslims here?"

"Not a lot," he answered. "I think they form about ten to fifteen percent of the Indian population in Fiji."

"Several weeks ago two guys were found dead in Seattle. They were not the usual shooting victims. Both had had their throats cut. They were almost decapitated. They had tattoos that a computer search suggested were of South Pacific origin. We don't have a lot of Fijians in the Seattle area, but there is quite a community in Vancouver, BC. We put the word out in both cities, but nobody turned up missing and we were back to square one."

"So you decided to drop by and have a look around in Fiji?"

"There's a little more to it," went on McCann.

"At the same time there was a bomb threat received at the Seattle airport. The whole area was closed up. A 747 was evacuated, and a device was found in a piece of carry-on baggage, but it turned out to be a fake. However, in the bag was a note stating that a real bomb would be set off in a crowded place in Seattle in the next few weeks if demands were not met. The mayor is to be informed as to these demands in a further communication at a later date. It all ended with 'Allah be praised' and was signed 'The Islamic World Federation.'"

McCann paused to finish his beer before continuing.

"There was also one other thing about the bag. It had a sliver of a sticker on the handle which was from an airline baggage tag and which we later traced to Air Pacific."

"Why didn't they make any demands in the original note, and why are they waiting to inform you of what they want in 'a further communication'?" Peter asked as he resumed his seat.

"We have no idea why," McCann shrugged. "But we better find out more about these guys and pretty soon." He paused and then went on.

"Do you know what a 'fatwa' is?"

"Oh, yes. I read the papers even here. A fatwa consists of a religious edict, and Muslim militants have issued a fatwa blessing attacks on U.S. citizens and the Jews. But I can't believe it's coming this far. Fiji's the last place I'd associate with that kind of thing."

Peter Barclay got up and walked to the window. "This is a nightmare. Where does it go from here?"

"Have you heard any anti-American sentiments being expressed publicly here recently?"

"There have been a couple of letters to the editor in the *Fiji Times* over the past while with comments about the U.S. being 'The Great Satan' and how the Americans are abusing the people of Iraq and Iran and Muslims elsewhere in the world. I was told to ignore them, as they were written by some nut and that the vast majority of the people of Fiji thought of America as their country's friend."

"He may be some nut," responded McCann, "but one nut can create a lot of dissension, and he is probably far from alone and may be joined by others who want to be blessed by the fatwa."

"So where do we go from here?" asked Peter.

"I don't know about you, Doc, but right now I'm going to bed," said McCann, swilling down the rest of his beer.

FOUR

McCann was awake before dawn. It was not daylight that penetrated his slumber, but the birds. There must have been a thousand of them outside.

McCann remounted his barstool of the night before, and Peter poured him a cup of black coffee. "Let's go outside, Detective," he said. As they came out on to the patio, the sky was a flurry of wings.

"You sure have it tough around here," said McCann. "It's easy to understand why you'd retire to this part of the world."

Peter looked across the pool toward the blaze of flowers on the other side of the garden.

"I don't miss the big city or its problems. The kind of problems you're bringing with you."

Peter turned back to face the detective. "Where do we go from here?"

The cop took a sip of his coffee. "I got a job to do. A big job, maybe. It seems to me that I need some local help, but I don't want you in the way."

"You think I probably know somebody you could talk to?" McCann looked at Peter.

"Well, do you know someone like that? It would help me get the job done and keep you out of this."

"I play golf with a guy who is in the detective squad of the Fiji police. He's a good guy. I think he would keep his mouth shut about you questioning him. Just so long as it didn't involve any confidential information or anything that was against the law."

McCann shrugged. "I think you can trust me not to make any trouble, Doc."

"I hope you're right," Peter said. "I hope you're right."

Mere served them breakfast, which they ate in silence.

After they had finished eating, Peter reached for the cordless phone on the table and made a call to his detective friend. He arranged for a meeting at a restaurant in town, saying only that he would have a friend along who was visiting from America.

About eleven a.m. they climbed into Peter's Toyota 4Runner and headed east on the Queen's Highway for the trip from Pacific Harbour to Suva. They crossed over the bridge at the Navua River, passing further inland and continuing through the countryside to Lami,, where the road joined the coast again. From then on they were in the Suva suburbs, and the traffic volume increased until it was almost bumper to bumper by the time they were approaching the mid city area.

Eventually they turned into a car park, where Peter managed to find a place in the shade. When McCann got out of the air-conditioned car, the heat hit him. They crossed the parking lot and made their way along the crowded streets, Peter leading the way to the restaurant.

McCann was glad to feel the relief of cool air as they entered. The dining room was crowded, and most of the tables were taken. Peter obviously knew the owner, who greeted him and showed them to a booth on the far side of the room. "How about a beer?" asked Peter.

"I thought you'd never offer!" McCann grinned.

Peter waved down a passing waiter and ordered a couple of stubbies.

They were on their second beers when a tall Fijian entered. After looking around, he crossed to their booth and slid in alongside the doctor.

"Bula, Pete," he said. "Sorry I'm a bit late, but I had to finish up some paper work."

"That's okay," said Peter. "I always expect you to be on Fiji time. I want you to meet Gerry McCann from my old hometown of Seattle. Gerry, this is my very good friend, Dan Tukana."

Tukana also had a Fiji Bitter, and Peter asked about his golf game while McCann looked over the menu. He eventually joined the other two in their choice of the restaurant's special of the day, lamb curry.

"Gerry and you have a lot in common," said Peter. "That's why I thought you would like to meet him. He works with the Seattle Police Department, although he's incognito here."

The Fijian's eyes hardened. "And what brings you to our fair shores?"

"Would you believe me if I told you I'm a pathologist on vacation and came to visit my old friend, the good doctor?"

"No," Tukana said. "Otherwise our first meeting would have been more casual, like at the golf course or on a fishing trip. You're working and maybe you need a little local input."

Peter broke in, "He's got a serious problem in Seattle, Dan, which involves some Fijian citizens, and I thought you might be able to help him without too much fuss being made."

"Well, I make no promises, but I'm willing to hear what you have to say. I'll help you if I can. But if this thing crosses the line, Gerry, I don't make any promises to keep it from the Fijian authorities. Fair enough?"

"Fair enough," replied McCann. "I wouldn't expect anything else from any good cop."

Their food arrived and the three men continued with light chatter as they ate, the two policemen exchanging information on their jobs. Tukana had been in the detective division of the Fiji Police for many years. He had no special assignment. Sometimes it involved missing persons, and he was accustomed to searching computer records of the police and immigration departments when necessary.

McCann and Tukana seemed to hit it off well during their lunchtime conversation. The two Americans finished with coffee, and Tukana had tea.

McCann withdrew an envelope from his pocket. "I'm working this case. These murders were done in my town."

The Fijian took the photographs and looked at them for several moments.

"I don't know them. You think they might be from Fiji?"

McCann nodded. He offered several more pictures to Tukana. "These show their tattoos. The designs are thought to be of Pacific Islands origin, possibly Fijian."

Tukana spent a while inspecting the tattoo shots and again looked at the postmortem photographs.

"I'll look into things and see what I can come up with. That means a missing persons search, and in Fiji it can take a while. We don't have a very large population, only about eight hundred thousand. But our population is dispersed, and the record keeping is poor or nonexistent in many areas."

Again looking at the tattoo photos, Tukana said, "The tattoos won't be found on a computer program either. The only thing I can suggest is talking to some of the older men in the villages who might recall these particular designs. That might lead to the region where these men came from." He turned to the doctor.

"You could try Ratu Timoci, Pete. Isn't he an old friend of yours from your fishing trips? He probably knows a great deal about Fijian tattooing and might be able to help you."

Peter nodded. "I'll give him a try. It'll give us the chance for a trip on the *Noqui Tau*, and I'm sure Gerry wouldn't mind the excuse for a little fishing."

FIVE

Special Agent John Kerrigan, FBI, left his apartment in the Leschi district. He headed along the shore of Lake Washington on Lakeside Avenue South, turning left on Lake Washington Boulevard and then up the winding road to the crest of the hill. He continued west and descended towards downtown Seattle.

Kerrigan was forty-five years old, married for twenty-five years to his wife, Marcy, and twenty-eight years to the Bureau. Two more and he was out. He was looking forward to a good pension and the chance for consulting work.

He went up the hill and entered the parking garage of the Jackson Federal Building, which fronted at 915 Second Avenue.

Taking the elevator to the seventh floor, he entered the headquarters of the Seattle Division of the FBI. He waved a greeting at the front desk and made his way back to where his partner, Barney Fisher, was already seated on the other side of the desk that they shared.

Kerrigan tossed his hat on top of a filing cabinet. "Mornin' ,Fish. How's it going?"

"Hi, Jack, it's going fine," responded Fisher, glancing up briefly.

"There's more action on the terrorist thing this morning, the embassy bombings in Nairobi, Kenya and in Dar es Salaam, Tanzania. There have been over 250 killed and thousands injured, some Americans as well as locals."

"Yeah, I've been hearing about it on the radio and TV. Holy shit, Fish! It gets worse all the time. Is there anything yet on the people involved? I suppose it's the Islamic extremists again?"

"The word is that our old friend, Osama bin Laden, is behind both bombings and they have several suspects in mind— guys who were known to be taught their art in Afghanistan at one of bin Laden's training camps for terrorists there."

Kerrigan poured himself a cup of coffee from the carafe across the room and returned to his chair, sitting down heavily.

"Bin Laden—very rich and very dedicated to waging a holy war against America. He has so much influence in Muslim countries and especially with the young hotheads."

"You got that right. But the trouble is that our embassies are no longer safe in any country, not just Muslim countries. There was a report about some Arab guys casing our embassy in Oslo. That's Norway, for Christ's sake. How Muslim is that? How can we cover all the U.S. installations around the world and protect them from these maniacs?"

Kerrigan sipped his coffee, thinking about the reams of reports and information gone over time and again. America's most dangerous enemy. The youngest son of a Saudi construction magnate, Muhammad bin Laden, of Yemeni origin, was founder of the bin Laden Group, which was worth some five billion dollars. Born in 1957 in the city of Riyadh, Osama bin Laden's personal wealth was estimated to be over 300 million dollars.

In 1979 bin Laden funded a volunteer force of Arab nationals to fight alongside the Afghan mujahedin after the

Soviets invaded Afghanistan. This group, called "The Islamic Salvation Front," was aided by the U.S. at the time of the Soviet invasion. In 1989, with the Soviet Union forced out of Afghanistan, the U.S. aid withdrawn and the unit disbanded, bin Laden returned to the family construction business.

After being accused of financing subversive activities by Egypt, Algeria and Yemen, the Saudi government seized his passport, and he fled to Sudan and the National Islamic Front. He was behind the organization of terrorist training camps in Sudan, but in May 1996 the axe fell again and the Sudanese expelled him for "harming the image of the country."

Osama bin Laden dedicated himself to waging a holy war, or Jihad, against the United States. He convened a meeting of fundamentalist extremists and sponsors of terrorism. A group of more than 150 clerics, "The International Islamic Front for the Jihad against Jews and Americans," issued a number of fatwas. They not only hated foreigners, but intended to depose Arab governments which do not follow the doctrine of Islamic extremism.

Kerrigan reviewed his list of bin Laden's past moves against the U.S:

1993—Supplied troops and rocket launchers that shot down U.S. helicopters in Mogadishu, Somalia, killing 18 servicemen.

1993—Connected to the World Trade Center bombing that killed six people and injured over 1000.

1995—Behind the bombing of a Saudi base in Riyadh that killed five Americans and two Indians and injured 60 people, including 34 Americans.

1998—Associated with Islamic groups claiming responsibility for the bombing of a U.S. Air Force housing complex at a base near Dhahran, Saudi Arabia, which killed 19 servicemen and injured over 300 others.

Osama bin Laden was also suspected of involvement in other terrorist acts:

1992—Hotel bombings in Yemen targeting U.S. servicemen on their way to Somalia as part of a UN force.

1993—Attempted assassination of Crown Prince Abdullah of Jordan.

1995—Attempted assassination of Egyptian President Mubarak in Sudan.

1996—Egyptian embassy bombing in Pakistan that killed 17 people.

Kerrigan sighed as he replaced the papers on the desk and got up to get another cup of coffee.

"Well, if they knew where to find the son of a bitch, they'd have him. My guess is he's not in Afghanistan or Pakistan. Christ, he could be sipping something sweet poolside in Miami."

The day's routine changed for the partners in mid morning when they were called to the office of the Special Agent in Charge of the Seattle Office, George Paxton. He was a tall, middle-aged man of imposing stature whose military bearing reflected his years in the Marine Corps prior to his FBI career. He was a disciplinarian, but commanded respect from his staff because he was open to suggestions.

Paxton looked up as the two men entered.

"Jack, Fish," he greeted them. "Close the door and sit down."

They sat in the two chairs across the desk from their boss.

"I just heard from DC that we have a visitor arriving at Seatac this afternoon. He's of interest to us and to you two in particular. His name's Sayed Naida, and he is suspected of being one of the terrorists involved in the Nairobi embassy attack. He's on a British Airways flight from London. The Brits spotted him arriving at Heathrow and tailed him to the transit lounge. As the plane was boarding, he met up with two other guys the Brits knew were involved in Islamic terrorist activities. They wanted us to have him, so as he was heading out on the BA flight, they made no attempt at arrest."

"Sounds like we're having a convention of these animals, what with the bomb threat and murders of last month and now this," Kerrigan said. "How do you want us to handle it?"

"Carefully, and with as little fuss as possible. We know how dangerous these people are and how little respect they have for human life, including their own. We want them taken when they land without anyone getting killed." He paused. "Especially the civilians."

"That's going to be a good trick at the airport with hundreds of people around," Fisher said.

"You're right. We do have a picture of the primary suspect emailed from London," said Paxton, pushing a photograph towards the two men. "However, we won't know the others except for a guess on their general appearance."

"We'll also have a little help from on board," he added. "An English cop who's stuck with this guy from Heathrow. Here's his picture too. Name is Timson."

"One of you had better contact the Seatac Airport security people," continued Paxton. "Let them know about this, but they've got to keep it quiet and not spread a bunch of uniforms around to make it too obvious that something's going down." Paxton stood up, which meant that the meeting was over.

"No Rambo stuff out there," he added as they went out the door.

Kerrigan and Fisher returned to their desk. Fisher got Al Bostwick, who handled Seatac security, on the phone. He said they'd need a half-dozen agents along with his people. Kerrigan said they'd be at the airport in an hour, which would give them three more hours to setup.

They discussed the situation with Paxton, who listened to their ideas and agreed with their plan, suggesting their primary back-up be agents Ben Molson and Ann Eaton. Kerrigan and Fisher had worked with these two before and felt comfortable with it. Paxton then called for the other two to join them and apprised them of the job ahead.

Molson was a redheaded import from Brooklyn and was known for his smart-aleck sense of humor that sometimes irked his boss. Today, however, he was quiet as Paxton told of the incoming terrorists. Ann Eaton was not only a good-looking woman, she was a damn good agent.

Paxton distributed copies of the photos from London to each of them and gave Kerrigan extras for the Seatac cops. They decided to put Molson and Eaton in the immigration lounge to mingle with the arriving passengers. Kerrigan would be in the arrival lounge at the customs area with Fisher. Paxton planned to be on the visitors' balcony overlooking the arrivals area, where he hoped he could see everyone. The other agents would be at the international gate and in the baggage area.

Fisher and Kerrigan briefed the other agents, then they left for the airport in three cars. The rain started as they left the Federal Building and steadily increased as they curved up the on ramp to the freeway going south.

Once in the airport complex, they came to the office buildings and parked outside the one that housed Airport Security. Bostwick met them. "I hope you have this thing under control. I've always enjoyed working with the Bureau, but I don't want any shooting in my airport. Get clear of here and then pick them up."

Paxton glared at the Seatac security chief and said, "Can we have a few words in your office?" Bostwick answered by going out the door, leaving it open behind him.

"Bostwick, I don't want any trouble with you. I want you to understand that, like you, I want this thing to be handled as quietly and with as little fuss as possible. Now hear this. My orders are from Washington, DC, and from as high up as it gets. This terrorist sonofabitch that we have to grab has been responsible for a lot of innocent lives being lost. He may be here to set up a blood bath in Seattle. Now we're going out into that other room to try to get this group organized as a cohesive unit to do the job. You can help us, and you know the territory. Are you on board? If not, stay out of the fucking way."

SIX

After a strained discussion in the conference room, the group was taken over to the arrival level of the airport in vans provided by Bostwick's people. They were escorted though the security area in the A concourse, bypassing the x-ray surveillance and metal detection equipment with their weapons and radios. They rode the tram out to the international arrivals area in the South Satellite, and there they dispersed to their various assigned posts.

Bostwick's men were at the tram platforms, at the international arrivals area, and in the main terminal. He also had others at the intermediate stops in case the terrorists tried to create a diversion or attempted to split up. Copies of the pictures had been provided to all in the group.

Molson and Eaton made their way to the immigration lounge and waited to mingle with passengers as they came though the ramp door off the aircraft. They were to try to get somewhere behind Naida and his friends.

The agents were to keep alert for any signals from the English lawman and hoped that he would be able to indicate how many bad guys there were and possibly to point them out in the crowd, since they only had pictures of Sayed Naida and Timson but not of the other terrorists.

Kerrigan and Fisher were in the customs baggage area. They had an hour before the passengers would filter through from immigration tion and begin to search for their baggage on the carousels. Each man had been checking the area, noting the doors and the possible escape routes for anyone trying to make a hurried exit. They had made themselves known to the customs officers on duty in case they had to make a dive through an inspection line.

Up on the balcony overlooking the customs baggage area, George Paxton was surveying the scene. Already some people were gathering around him as they prepared to greet passengers off the BA flight from London. Paxton kept his gaze neutral.

The 747 landed and taxied to the gate. The sound of the fan jets could be heard in the building, and as the whine decreased, the anticipation within the waiting group increased. The doors at the gate opened.

The passengers emerged, some looking tired and others quite bright after the ten-hour flight. They were shepherded into lines before the immigration officers' desks, standing behind the red marks as directed by the signs. There were lines of "Non-U.S. Citizens" and lines of "U.S. Citizens Only." They lengthened as passengers exited in increasing numbers.

Molson, Eaton, and their back-ups waited around the exit doors from the aircraft ramps, one on each side of the gate area. Eventually Naida emerged at the door from the forward end of the plane. They recognized him easily from the photograph. They were more concerned now with spotting the others, but had no way to identify them.

Sayed Naida had a swarthy appearance and might have been a stereotype of an Islamic terrorist. He was about five feet nine inches tall and had a black beard and mustache. He was wearing a light tan colored suit and a brown shirt with no necktie. He continued to the immigration area and joined one of the lines assigned to foreign citizens. Ann Eaton joined in the same line, with two couples in between Naida and herself.

Ben Molson continued to wait by the ramp exits until he recognized the English officer coming through the doors. He fell in alongside him and quietly identified himself. The Brit, Timson, appeared to ignore him and kept on walking towards immigration. As they got in a crowd of people where the lines started to form, he turned around in Molson's direction and asked, "Have you people spotted Naida?"

Molson said "Yeah, my partner's on him up ahead. Can you identify his friends?"

"They were near the back of the aircraft when I took a stroll around earlier, but I haven't seen them since then. Maybe we should hang back to see if we can find them coming out late."

"Okay, but I gotta let the boss know what's going on." He knelt down by a bag he had been carrying and, pretending to rummage through its contents, called quietly on the radio to George Paxton. "This is Molson. Eaton is behind Naida in the left alien line. I'm with the Brit at the back of the immigration hall. We're hanging here trying to spot the other bad guys."

Up on the balcony, Paxton heard the message through his earpiece. He showed no indication that anything was being said, but tapped twice on his sending button to let Molson know his message had been received. He then let Kerrigan and Fisher know that Eaton had Naida ahead of her and that Molson was with Timson.

Ann Eaton followed her man in the line with the two couples between them and let him proceed to the desk, making no effort to interfere. She waited her turn and, on reaching the desk, presented her FBI identification to the immigration officer, who let her proceed through to the customs area. She knew that Kerrigan and Fisher would be waiting to pick up their man there.

Meanwhile, Molson and the Brit were maintaining their position by the exit doors. Timson said quietly "There's one of them now—the fellow in the navy jacket at the far door."

Molson said quickly, "Got him—where's the other one?"

Timson looked around. "Don't know. Can't see any sign of him yet."

"Okay," said Molson. "I'll stick with the navy jacket and you get on to the other one when you spot him. We'll be keeping an eye on you as you follow him."

Molson moved off. They went along with the other passengers, and eventually the suspect got in the same line used by Naida. Molson got behind him with several other passengers in between. Between the immigration desk and the customs hall, Molson again radioed to let Paxton know that he was tailing one of Naida's associates and that Timson was behind him looking for the second one.

Timson waited until the passengers had stopped exiting the doors from the aircraft. Then he went down the ramp back to the aircraft, where he asked a cabin attendant if all the passengers were off the plane yet.

"All gone, sir, nobody left aboard except for some crew," said the man. "Are you missing one of your friends?"

"Yes. Thank you. I'll probably find him up ahead somewhere."

He turned around and was headed back up the ramp when he heard somebody behind him ask, "Has anyone seen my hat and jacket? They were hanging right here in the closet."

Timson wheeled around and saw one of the stewards looking in a closet near the exit door. The closet was close to several lavatories at the front of the business class section.

"When did you last see your jacket?" Timson asked the attendant, adding, "I'm with the police."

"It was there just before we landed," said the crewman. "Christ, mate, you chaps are really on the job…"

Timson ran back up the ramp, reentering the immigration hall. He searched the crowd in front of him, but saw no sign of his quarry. He had also lost Molson, who had already moved through to the customs area in behind the other suspect. He saw no uniformed crew members. The missing terrorist would have changed out of the stolen clothes in one of the immigration hall restrooms.

In the customs area the baggage was clattering onto the carousel, and the passengers were crowded around with carts ready to grab their baggage and get in line for customs inspection. It was difficult to spot someone now that they were milling around.

Kerrigan and Fisher had picked out Naida as he came through into the customs baggage area. They also noted that Eaton was in a group of people entering just behind the terrorist. She was chatting with one of the women beside her.

Naida collected a baggage cart from a rack at the side of the building and pushed it towards the carousel. The agents were anxious to identify the bags he would collect. The dark man moved behind the people crowding around the carousel, making no effort to push in and draw attention to himself.

Timson kept searching through the passengers as the immigration lines became shorter, noting his man was not to be found there. He went to the front and, presenting his credentials to the supervising officer standing near one of the desks, was quickly processed through. He hurried along to the customs hall to search for Molson, the only friendly face he would know.

Molson, meanwhile, was sticking close to his assignment. Fisher picked him out. Molson nodded at the terrorist suspect. Fisher looked at the man and nodded back.

Kerrigan was backing up Eaton and had moved over to get close to Naida's other side. He was still looking around, keeping an eye open for his partner and Molson and hoping to get to see their suspect as well.

Timson came into the customs hall quickly and started searching for Molson. He was moving around in the crowds by the carousels when Fisher, who had recognized him from his photograph, approached him.

"Fisher, FBI. Did you spot your man?"

"No. I couldn't find him anywhere and have no idea where he is. He might now be wearing an airline attendant's jacket." He continued to look around the hall as he spoke.

"Keep looking. I'll spread the word about the jacket."

Kerrigan was still looking in Naida's direction and saw that Eaton was close behind the terrorist. Moving back towards them, Kerrigan let Paxton know that the third terrorist was still unaccounted for.

Naida moved through the people at one of the carousels to grab a suitcase that he placed on his baggage cart. He then turned back, looking for more luggage. This turned out to be a duffel bag. He placed it on the cart. He then pushed the cart towards one of the lines for customs inspection. The customs examination was cursory, the inspectors asking some questions but opening very few bags. Naida was not delayed by the officer taking his declaration form. He pushed his cart along to leave his luggage to be forwarded to the baggage claim area at the front of the airport.

Unnoticed by Eaton, who was behind him, the terrorist had slipped a package out of the duffel bag and hidden it inside his jacket. He then headed out the exit to join the throng of people waiting on the platform to take the tram to the main terminal, Eaton and Kerrigan following along behind.

On the platform Eaton stayed close to Naida, who was near one of the two tram entrance doors. Kerrigan moved closer to the second door further along the platform. Naida was able to unwrap the loose packaging from around the pistol inside his jacket.

The tram arrived and the doors opened, disgorging a number of passengers. People started to board, and Eaton followed Naida into the tram. The swarthy man moved along the inside of the tram towards the second door. She was afraid that following him would make her too obvious, so she stayed where she had boarded. Kerrigan was ready to enter through the other door as it started to close, when just at that moment, Naida jumped out. Kerrigan twisted around and, regaining his footing with difficulty, started after the terrorist.

Naida ran along a corridor towards stairs leading up to an office area. Kerrigan called into his radio that he was in pursuit of the main terrorist but could not tell them exactly where he was headed.

At the bottom of the stairs Naida spun around, dropping to one knee as he pulled out the pistol and rapidly fired three shots at Kerrigan.

The first slug hit the agent in the stomach and the other two in the chest. Kerrigan got off one shot that missed widely, and he was already dying as he hit the ground.

SEVEN

The shots were heard up in the observation balcony, and George Paxton had a sudden sinking feeling, knowing that things had gone sour and not knowing which of his people was involved. He rushed out the door towards the escalator, shouting into the radio as he ran along.

"What's going on? Kerrigan? Fisher? Somebody answer!"

He reached the escalator and started down, still running down the steps. Fisher's voice came through on the radio. It sounded choked up and hoarse.

"This is Fisher. I've found Kerrigan. He's down in a corridor near the platform."

Paxton got back on the radio and told Bostwick that Naida was loose somewhere in the airport and to seal off the area where Kerrigan was down.

Eaton came back on the next tram.

"Okay, Ann, what happened?"

All she could tell him was that Naida had jumped out the far door of the tram as it was closing and, as it pulled away, she caught a glimpse of Kerrigan turning to run after him.

Paxton turned to Fisher. "Get back out there and back up Molson. Arrest that sonofabitch that he's following as soon as you get him in a good place."

Fisher went out the door and retraced his steps through the exit door of the customs hall. He spotted Molson behind his man, who had just passed the inspector's desk. Fisher signaled to Molson, and the other agent nodded. They both moved in on the terrorist suspect.

"FBI. You're under arrest!" said Fisher abruptly.

No resistance was offered, and they walked him into a room at the back of the building which the customs officials used for searches. While Fisher stood by, Molson handcuffed the suspect, checked his English, then read him his rights and checked for weapons. The man gave his name as Ali Saleem and claimed to be a Pakistani citizen living in London.

The search for Naida and the third terrorist blanketed the South Satellite and main terminal. The bags belonging to Naida and the one suspect who had been apprehended were taken to a security room in the baggage claim area. Unclaimed baggage from the flight would also be inspected.

Paxton went to the room where Fisher and Molson had their man under arrest. Timson was also there.

Paxton glared at Saleem and then turned towards Timson.

"I'm George Paxton, Special Agent in Charge of the Seattle FBI office. Pleased to meet you, Detective Sergeant Timson."

"And I you, sir."

"I take it that you can identify this man as one of the two who were seen with Naida at Heathrow?"

"Yes sir," said Timson, "and I'm only too sorry that we appear to have lost the other one. He appears to have given us the slip by masquerading as a flight attendant to get off the aircraft."

"Yeah. It looks like they may have made it out of the airport. Otherwise we should have taken them by now. Perhaps we can prevail upon you to stay around a little longer while we interrogate this one and go through their baggage."

Timson nodded.

Paxton turned back to Fisher and Molson. "Get this character out of here and make sure you keep a tight rein on him. His friends could make a move to break him loose. No escapes, no suicides–got it?"

He nodded to Fisher and walked him to the back of the room.

"How's it going, Fish? This is toughest for you, I know. I'll be calling his wife and son as soon as I can."

"Why couldn't it have been me instead of him?" Fisher stared blankly at the wall. "I don't have any family to worry about me or to worry about."

Paxton moved on, checking by radio with Bostwick, asking him to meet him in the BA baggage claims area.

Fisher, Molson and Timson surrounded the handcuffed terrorist, and the group left the interrogation room. They boarded the tram for the main terminal. Fisher had called for one of the FBI vehicles to be brought around outside the BA arrivals area.

As they moved between the carousels, there was a single gunshot from near the top of the escalator leading to the garage sky bridge.

Terrorist Ali Saleem slumped to the ground between the three law officers, blood oozing from a hole where his left eye had been.

The shooter had dropped the rifle and was running across the sky bridge, people scattering out of his way as they saw the pistol in his hand.

Once inside the garage, he leapt through the open door of a waiting Buick. It screamed off in the direction of the exit but, after turning a corner, the car made another turn back into the parking sections. It pulled into an empty space. The occupants got out and walked quickly to a green Dodge, parked several lanes away. The Dodge backed out and slowly followed the traffic lanes to the garage exit, where it entered the flow of vehicles leaving the airport.

Fisher had run for the escalator, hotly pursued by Molson, who hollered to Timson to stay with Saleem. One of Bostwick's men ran over to Timson and another ran in the same direction as the FBI men. The one with Timson called the medics.

The pursuit through the sky bridge and into the garage failed. Fisher and Molson found people who had seen a bearded man with a pistol jumping into a light colored Buick sedan, which tore off in the direction of the exit, but then it was lost from sight as it rounded the corner. No one had a good look at the driver, who was wearing sunglasses, and they saw no one else in the car. One astute young man had noted the license number. Molson put out an APB on a light colored Buick sedan. Bostwick's man radioed airport security, and they dispatched a car to the freeway exit.

Fisher radioed the bad news to Paxton. The FBI chief and Bostwick reached Timson and the slain terrorist as Fisher and Molson returned. Molson knelt by the body and removed the handcuffs.

"Shit," he said.

Bostwick had the medics cover the body on a stretcher. It was taken into a room at the back of the baggage claim area, ready for the King County morgue.

Bostwick turned to Paxton and said "Well, I guess that's about all that's going to happen to screw up things around here for today. We didn't do too well, did we?"

Paxton glared at him, and then his face relaxed. "No, we didn't do too well. I lost one of the best agents in the Bureau and a good friend, and we no longer have a suspect to interrogate. You've got your job to do, and I understand that. But this thing is a long ways from being over and, like it or not, you're still in the middle of it—maybe as much as we are."

The FBI chief left with Fisher, Molson and Timson.

Back at his office in the Federal Building, Paxton got on the phone to call Mrs. Kerrigan. Two agents would go out to see her, and he himself would go tomorrow morning.

Paper work now occupied the agents, as all had to write reports. Timson was also requested to give a detailed statement regarding his part in the operation from its start at London's Heathrow to his arrival at the Federal Building.

Paxton dictated his report carefully and thoroughly, as he knew Bostwick would be doing the same. There would be an investigation into the procedures at the airport today. Some on the investigating committee would consider the operation a fiasco that reflected on the FBI.

Paxton made a call to the King County medical examiner's office. Dr. Bill Childers was sitting in his office with a cup of coffee in his hand, just back from checking on two autopsies of murder victims. He didn't waste words as he answered the phone.

"Hi George, I got the word about your action at the airport. Sorry to hear about Kerrigan. He was well liked."

"It was a blow to lose him like that. He was a good man." Paxton paused. "You'll be getting the slugs from us, but right now we don't have a weapon to match them to."

"Just you get that bastard. Any leads?"

"Oh we know who he is—a terrorist connected with the embassy bombings in Africa. But right now we've no idea where to find him. He disappeared after the shooting. I want you to go over the other one with a fine tooth comb. He was our only chance for information, and his own people took him out. Anything you can give us might be our only lead."

"We'll do what we can, George. Is there anything in particular that you're looking for, or maybe expecting me to find?"

"Not a thing. It's just that it's our only hope. I know you'll do your best."

EIGHT

The rifle was gone over carefully by FBI firearms experts. It gave up nothing. It was a Kalishnikov with an ordinary sport scope attachment. Identifying numbers had been chemically removed, and there were no prints on the rifle, cartridges or magazine. Nearby a golf club travel bag had been found. It had been used to transport the weapon. The bullet that killed the terrorist showed a match with the rifle.

The Buick with the identifying license number was soon found in the parking garage. It had been stolen from a Southcenter Mall parking lot that afternoon, and it revealed nothing.

Paxton called for his secretary to come into his office. "Pam, I want you to get the Special Counter-Terrorist Squad together for a meeting as soon as possible. See when they can all fit it in and let me know how soon we can meet. Okay?"

"Very good, Mr. Paxton. I'll get on it right away." After making several calls, she knocked on Paxton's door to give him the time of the meeting: that evening at seven.

Paxton called the airport group into his office—Fisher, Molson, Eaton and also Timson. They discussed the operation from their arrival at the airport until their return to the FBI headquarters. Each agent and the British policeman went over his or her movements and was pressed to offer the reasoning for the actions taken. There was much discussion, but no blame.

Before dismissing the group, Paxton told them to be available on their cell phones in case they were needed for questioning by the Special Counter-Terrorist Squad later. He also asked Timson for his cooperation in this regard and knew he could get him through Molson.

Paxton blamed himself for mismanaging the operation and knew that his FBI superiors would be critical of his handling of it. He also anticipated the Secret Service and CIA would be upset about not being consulted and involved in the planning. Paxton turned back to the paper work and continued to sweat over his report. The blame lay with him for John Kerrigan's death. And he would be held responsible for the escape of Sayed Naida and his fellow terrorist.

An hour before the meeting was scheduled, he left the office and went down the street to a café, where he had a sandwich and a cup of coffee. After a second coffee, he made his way back to his office. Gathering up his and the airport team's reports, he went to the conference room.

Len Williams of the CIA was the first to arrive. He gave Paxton a cordial enough greeting.

"Hi George, how's it going?"

"About like you'd expect."

Williams took a seat next to Paxton, who was at the head of the table.

"Sorry about Kerrigan."

"Yeah. Well, I'll be giving you the whole story when everyone arrives."

Ron Marsh of the Secret Service entered, followed in by Mat Benson, a captain with the Seattle Police Department.

"Hello George, Len," said Marsh. Benson also mumbled "George, Len," as the two took their places at the table.

"Okay, let's get to it," said Paxton. "Thanks for coming at short notice like this but you know it's urgent." The three men said nothing.

"I'll give you my rundown on the day's happenings at the airport and then answer your questions. My people are on call if you have to question any of them."

For the next thirty to forty minutes, Paxton went over the FBI actions from the first notification of the impending arrival of the terrorists on BA Flight 49 until the return of the group to the Federal Building. His listeners made occasional notes.

When he had finished, the first to speak was Len Williams of the CIA. "I'm sure the first thing we all want to know is why none of us was informed that this thing was going down so we could be involved in it. I thought this group was formed for that very purpose. The CIA takes a dim view of this lack of communication, George."

"There wasn't a lot of time to get a conference together on procedure," Paxton said. "This was considered to be an FBI operation and in our jurisdiction. I also thought that the more complicated we made it by involving different agencies, the more difficult it would be to quickly plan the course of action." He waited.

"Well, it doesn't seem to have worked too smoothly—the operation," continued Williams. "And maybe it would have worked better with more input from other terrorism experts."

Paxton snapped back, "I don't think anyone here has had too much experience in arresting a foreign terrorist in our own back yard. Just how would you have handled it differently?"

Williams reddened. "Whatever it took to do the job. I'd have picked up Naida as he exited the plane and not fooled around in the immigration or customs halls."

"You're not thinking clearly about the situation, Len," said Paxton, regaining his composure. "We didn't know if

Naida was armed or if he had an armed accomplice in the area. We hadn't yet identified his pals who had boarded with him in London. We simply couldn't take the chance that other passengers could get hurt at that stage."

Mat Benson broke into the tense silence.

"I understand that George had to wait for a safer move, but I agree we should all have known about this thing at the planning stage."

Ron Marsh spoke for the first time. "It would seem that so far everyone is right, and I can't argue with any of you." He paused to look around at each of them in turn. "George, you had to move fast on this thing, but you could have informed us that it was going down. Maybe one of us might have had further information through our own agencies about this Naida and his friends that might have been useful. Maybe we could have given you backup without interfering in the operation." He paused, doodling on his notepad.

"Anyhow, we know that George feels bad enough about things, what with Kerrigan's death and the escape of these terrorists. We can come back to this, but we need to get on with the overall question of terrorism in the Seattle area. Now, how does this Naida fit into that?"

Williams looked at Marsh. "He has to be related to the group that were involved in the bomb threat at Seatac. It looks like there might be a whole gang of these people in this area now, and they seem to be hatching something big if they're bringing in a guy from the Nairobi bombing."

Paxton was depressed. The failure to capture Naida looked more and more like it would lead to disaster. He asked the obvious question. "Has anyone got anything new on the Islamic extremists since we had our last meeting?"

Williams said that the CIA had intel and rumors on groups coming in all the time, but they had nothing new that related to the Seatac bomb threat or to the Seattle area. Marsh had nothing to report from the Secret Service.

Captain Benson spoke up again. "Well, I should tell you about Gerry McCann."

"What's he up to?" Paxton asked.

Benson looked somewhat awkward, if not embarrassed.

"After the airport bomb threat thing, a couple of black guys were found dead in a park in the Rainier district. They'd both had their throats cut. They had tattoos that might have been from the South Pacific. In addition to that, there was a piece of Air Pacific baggage tag found on the bag that contained the fake bomb at Seatac."

Benson had the full attention of the group, who were all staring at him.

"McCann thought he ought to look into things in Fiji, which is where Air Pacific flies to. And Fiji has a big Muslim population."

Williams erupted again. "Does anyone in this group share information? What the hell is going on here? How come McCann didn't let us know about this? And more importantly, what's he doing outside of Seattle? He's way off the reservation."

"He said he wanted to look into things quietly without rocking the boat and making a big political stink in Fiji."

"Does he have a cover at least?" asked Paxton.

"He contacted a doctor down there who is a friend of Bill Childers, the M.E. He's there like he's a doctor on a holiday."

"Has he come up with anything? Have you heard from him yet?" asked the CIA man. "You're on the hook for him."

"He's only been gone a few days, and he's doing his investigation."

This latest revelation was discussed for a while, and after each man made his comments, they reached consensus. It was unanimous that someone else should be sent to Fiji to work with McCann. This individual should be a representative of one of the federal agencies and should not pose a threat to McCann's cover. McCann should turn his operation over as soon as he could safely extricate himself.

Paxton proposed Ann Eaton for the second undercover person. She could travel as McCann's girlfriend joining him on holiday. Williams and Marsh each wanted to send someone from his own agency, but neither wanted to get into the existing mess. And neither could deny Eaton's ability and experience.

They would have to move quickly.

NINE

The *Noqui Tau* moved past the hotel and along the channel to reach Beqa Lagoon. The sun was shining, and there was no threat of rain this early in the day. The wind came up and the boat began to rock a little as they moved away from the shelter of the breakwater.

Peter was in his chair at the wheel and pushed the throttles forward as they reached the open water, the twin diesels responding smoothly.

Standing beside him, Detective McCann was looking ahead at the island of Beqa to the south and further to the west, the smaller island of Yanuca.

Beqa was about seven nautical miles away in a south-southeasterly direction from the entrance to Pacific Harbour. The island was about fifteen square miles in area and mountainous, largely uninhabited except for some villages around the coast. It has a resort called Marlin Bay that caters largely to guests interested in scuba diving, for which Beqa Lagoon is world-renowned.

Peter turned around in his chair and waved to his deck-hand, Jone, who was readying a couple of fishing poles, one on each side of the afterdeck. He had the lures laid out with their colorful skirts flopping in the breeze.

"Okay Jone, let 'em out," Peter hollered. The big Fijian nodded and released the brake on the port side reel. They watched the lure run out to where it was skipping on the water about fifty to sixty yards astern. He did the same thing with the starboard rig, this time letting it out fifteen yards further.

Peter adjusted the boat's speed to set the action of the lures the way he wanted it. He then looked to Jone again. The boatman turned back to watch the lures and behind his back, held his thumb downwards. Peter pulled back slightly on the throttles until Jone signaled that he had the speed just right.

The course towards Beqa looked like it was a direct one as McCann looked over the bow and could see only uninter-rupted sea and waves ahead. But he noticed that Peter was keeping an eye on the depth finder and every so often would make a change in direction.

"Coral heads can be upon you unannounced," Peter said. "If you want to have a look, you'll find a chart in that locker beside you that shows the channels and reefs in the lagoon. We know them pretty well—at least in daylight—but I still keep an eye on the depth finder."

They continued across the lagoon towards Beqa and passed Marlin Bay Resort to port. Rounding the southwest point of Beqa with Ugaga Island off to starboard, they headed east inside the Kavukavu Reef, which is the Beqa barrier reef.

They passed several small bays, and Peter turned again to Jone to reel in the lines as they approached Daku Point. He backed off on the throttles as they rounded the point and entered Dakuibeqa Bay.

Peter turned to McCann as the boat slowed.

"This is the main village of the Sawau tribe. They're the famous firewalkers of Fiji. They also live in three other villages on this coast. The chief is Tui Sawau, and he lives here in Dakuibeqa. We've got to go through a welcoming ceremony before we can do anything else."

Jone moved up on the bow and got ready to lower the anchor as the boat slowly approached the village. The coral could be clearly seen, and Jone pointed ahead to direct Peter as the *Noqui Tau* edged her way through the reef. Peter put the boat in reverse briefly to bring her to a stop, and Jone heaved the anchor over the bow. He then backed up a little more to get the anchor to catch. Peter shut down the diesels, and the silence was interrupted only by the sound of the birds from shore and the lapping water.

A skiff came out from the beach in front of the village. By the time the anchor was secure, it was alongside and its only occupant, a young Fijian wearing a brightly colored sulu, called to them.

"Bula Pete, Bula Jone. It's good to see you."

The two men answered with "Bula" and, as the small boat came alongside, Peter said, "How are you doing, Phillip? Still chasing the girls around the village?"

Phillip grinned sheepishly. "Sure, Pete, do you want to join me?" The young man climbed aboard, shaking hands with Jone and Peter.

"Phillip, I want you to meet a friend of mine, Gerry McCann," said Peter, and the Fijian extended his hand. "Bula Gerry."

"This young stud is Phillip Kavoka, and he's one of the sons of my old friend that we've come to see, Ratu Timoci."

"You fellas just out fishing today, or are you up to something else?" Phillip's eyes were warm black in the sun.

"Well, we hoped to talk to the Ratu. Mac here is interested in finding out about some Fijian tattoo art. I thought maybe your father could help."

"You know he'll always be glad to help you if he can, Pete. He'll be pleased to see you again."

McCann collected his photos from the cabin, and the three men joined Phillip in his boat.

Jone was carrying a package, which to McCann looked like a bundle of dried roots. Peter nodded at it.

"That's kava. It's the root of a pepper plant. It's known in Fiji as yaqona. The people in Fiji and elsewhere in the South Pacific grind it up to a powder and make a drink from it. They use it for ceremonial purposes, but also drink it socially at every opportunity." Jone and Phillip were smiling again.

"We'll be presenting this as a gift to the chief, and we'll be seated with him in his bure while the presentation is made."

Phillip stood in the middle of the skiff and expertly poled it through the coral to the beach. Jone jumped off forward with the painter in his hand and hauled the bow up onto the sand as Phillip pushed with his pole. Peter and McCann moved forward and stepped off, carrying their shoes.

The four men walked up the beach to the entrance to the village, where the Americans donned their shoes. Then they walked between the bures and past the church to the chief's house. This was a large bure in the traditional Fijian style, with a thatched roof, in contrast to many of the others that were of cement block construction with corrugated tin roofs.

As they walked through the village, they were accompanied by young children who were staring at them and whispering. Singing could be heard coming from the school. At each doorway there were women and older men who smiled at them as they passed. The newcomers smiled and waved.

When they reached the door to the chief's bure, they removed their shoes, which they left outside. Phillip went in first and then stood to one side to let the others enter. They found a large single room that was cool and comfortable when they came in out of the hot sunshine. The floor was covered with large woven mats, and at the back of the room were the sleeping quarters with other matting. McCann noticed pictures of the Queen and other members of the British royal family placed high around the bure walls.

Before them sat the chief, Tui Sawau. On each side of the chief sat several elders of the village, including Ratu Timoci. All were seated cross-legged on the matted floor. Some women were seated further back in the room.

The chief was sitting behind the tanoa, a large bowl made of vesi, a Fijian hardwood. The tanoa was the "grog bowl" containing the muddy-appearing drink made from yaqona or kava root. Stretching from the tanoa and away from the chief was a thick rope made of coconut fronds, at the end of which was a cowrie shell. Phillip gestured for Peter to take his place before the cowrie shell, and the doctor sat down, cross-legged as were the Fijians. This location in the gathering made him the guest of honor. McCann and Jone sat slightly behind and on each side of Peter.

The ceremony was conducted in Fijian and began with much low voiced ritualistic talk between Phillip, who was representing the visitors, and the chief. The gift bundle was presented. There were frequent phrases spoken in unison by the other Fijians following the chief's comments or statements. One member of the group began mixing the yaqona in the bowl by stirring it with a cloth that he wrung out frequently.

Eventually the talking came to an end and a bilo, a half coconut shell, was filled and handed to Peter. He clapped his hands together once and took the bilo. After draining it without stopping, he said "Maca," which means, " t's empty." He then clapped three times after handing back the empty bilo.

The chief was the next to have a bilo, followed by McCann and Jone and then the other Fijians. From then on, they all took it in turns to drink, and the ceremonial occasion gave way to a social one. Peter introduced the chief to McCann, who was handling things well, although he thought that the taste of the yaqona was something that would take some getting used to. He got a bit cramped in the cross-legged position and gradually slid his legs to one side to sit on one hip.

After a time, the grog bowl was getting to be nearly empty, and Peter stood up to thank the chief and take his leave before it could be refilled.

Outside the bure they were joined by Timoci and Phillip, and they went to sit in the shade where, another kava bowl appeared and a bilo made its rounds again.

"We need your help, Ratu," said Peter. "This is confidential. My friend Gerry here is trying to find out about a couple of men who were killed in America. He thinks they came from Fiji. He's trying to locate their village and learn more about them. It's important."

"You don't know who the men were?" asked the Ratu.

"No," answered McCann. "Nor do we know why they were killed or who killed them."

Peter emptied another bilo and then turned back to Timoci. "We heard from Dan Tukana in Suva that you know about tattooing in Fiji. We have some pictures of these men's tattoos and wondered if they might suggest where they came from."

McCann handed over the photos one by one and Timoci studied them, handing back each with a grunt. "These men come from the Savusavu region. Try Dromoninuku village. The village chief is Samuela Nawaibalavu."

There was nothing more to learn from Timoci, and they left. Phillip ferried the three visitors back out to the *Noqui Tau*, and before he pushed off, Peter gave him another package of yaqona for his father.

TEN

They got back to Pacific Harbour in the late afternoon just as it was starting to rain, and as they passed under the highway bridge, the sky blackened, and Peter knew that they were in for a torrential downpour typical of Fiji. These rainstorms were usually an afternoon occurrence and sometimes were brief. But they could last for several hours. Jone had seen the storm approaching, and in addition to his usual arrival chores, had been busy closing windows and shutters before the rain began. Peter moved down from the flying bridge to the cabin steering station in anticipation of the dousing to come. Jone placed a heavy plastic cover over the seat and gear on the weather deck.

By the time they arrived at the dock, the rain was torrential and was described by McCann as "like a cow pissing on a flat rock."

Fortunately, Ramesh was waiting for them with several large golf umbrellas. They hustled up to the villa, where Mere was waiting inside the door with some towels. After drying off, Peter headed for the refrigerator and filled two glasses with ice and orange juice, to which he added the customary OP Fijian rum. He took the drinks into the living room, where McCann was sitting down, drying off his feet.

"Thanks," said the cop. "This will really hit the spot. Bula!"

Peter smiled. "Bula."

"I'll put in a call to Dan Tukana and let him know about our trip to Beqa," McCann said. "I'm anxious to get going on finding out more about these guys. Time could be running out, and those bastards may be about ready to follow up on their threat of setting off a big one in the Seattle area."

Peter reached for the phone and punched in the Suva number of the Fiji Police. He asked for Tukana, and after the detective came on the line, he put McCann on.

Tukana listened as McCann told him of the lead on the tattoos to the Savusavu region. "I'll call you back in a while. I have to check out a few things," he said.

Peter got on the computer to pick up his email messages. There were a couple from old friends which were of the "just saying hello" type, and he skipped through those. The third email was for McCann and was from Captain Benson.

The email from Benson was a long one and started with a summary of the airport action. McCann murmured a quiet "Holy shit!" as he read about the death of John Kerrigan, whom he had known for a lot of years. He couldn't believe that the FBI had lost a man at Seatac like this. The killing of the terrorist by his own people in the baggage claim area was not all that surprising to McCann, with his experience on the Counter-Terrorist Squad.

As he finished each page, he handed it over for Peter to read. The doctor's eyes widened as he read about the shootings. He now found himself more involved than ever in the whole affair. On the one hand, he resented the intrusion into his quiet life in Fiji, but he couldn't deny an exhilaration and excitement. Perhaps the quiet life had been getting too quiet.

Captain Benson went on to relate the outcome of the Special Counter-Terrorist Squad meeting, including the decision to send a federal agent to work in Fiji. McCann resented this. He didn't need any baby-sitting by the Feds, particularly by a female. This evoked another and louder "Holy shit!" It was to be Ann Eaton and she was due to arrive the following evening.

When they finished reading Benson's email, Peter said, "I can see why you're anxious to get moving on this thing."

McCann looked at Peter. "Doc, I don't think you should be involved. You can see how dangerous it is, and I've no right to put you in harm's way more than I already have. I'll just have to move to a hotel and take the chance on my cover elsewhere."

Peter stared at him. "Are you out of your mind? You could be under surveillance by these people already, and they would have no problem tracing you anywhere in this country. You need someone with local knowledge to help you get around. I won't hear of you making any dumb moves because of concerns for my safety. Anyhow, if they're onto you already, you can bet they must figure that I'm involved too."

McCann protested, but knew that Peter was right and that it was too late to protect him by leaving. "Okay. But I'm calling the shots, and you stay out unless I tell you different. No questions asked."

Peter didn't bother to reply. "Do you know this Ann Eaton?" he asked.

McCann nodded. "I've had some contact with her through liaison stuff, but I haven't worked with her on any projects. She has a good reputation as an agent, and from what I've heard she is very capable. But I don't give a damn who it is. I don't need a fed supervisor when I'm working and, after all, following this lead to Fiji was my idea."

Peter got the message and said no more. He pulled two stubbies from the fridge, and just then the phone rang. It was Dan Tukana.

"I've been going over some stuff on the computer and can't come up with anything about people missing from the Savusavu area. There's only one way to find out if someone has disappeared, and that's to go over there and ask questions. I'm going to make a trip to Savusavu on the eight-thirty plane tomorrow morning. It would be all right for your friend Mac and you to go along if you want."

"I'll tell Mac. It turns out that there was a fracas at the airport in Seattle. An FBI man was killed, as well as a terrorist off a plane from London. Things are heating up there, and McCann is really anxious to learn anything here that might help. He feels strongly that there is a Fiji connection to this mess."

"We got the word on the Seatac action already, but nobody here knows about anything related to Fiji. You can tell Mac that I'll respect his anonymity. But if we identify the dead guys found in Seattle, I must report it and also the probable Fiji connection to the Seatac action. Make sure he gets that clear."

"All right, Dan. But it'll be just the two of you. I've got things to do here. Anyhow, we'll pick you up about six-thirty and I'll take you to the airport. Okay?"

"Okay, my friend. *Moce*," said Tukana without argument and hung up.

Peter told the McCann about the trip he had arranged for him with Tukana. "I won't be going along," he said. "Someone has to pick up the FBI lady, and I guess I'm elected."

The storm passed overnight, and they were up early, leaving in the 4Runner for the run to Suva to pick up Tukana. It was a beautiful morning as they drove east into the rising sun, and Peter told McCann that he should be enjoying a nice flight to Savusavu. McCann was too involved with thoughts of the Seattle killings to have much interest in the lush green countryside with the bright red clay where cuts had been made in the hills.

As they neared the city, traffic increased and they found themselves in the dreaded Suva rush hour traffic jam. It was noisy and dirty, with clouds of black smoke coming from older buses and trucks.

Peter took a circuitous route to Tukana's office, trying to avoid the worst of the traffic. They found him waiting for them outside.

"*Nisa yadra*, Dan," Peter greeted him with the Fijian "Good morning."

"G'day Pete, Mac. How's it going?"

Tukana climbed in the back, and they nudged through the mess of city traffic to get on the road to the Nausori airport. This was one of the busiest routes into Suva, but fortunately they were heading out of the city in the morning when most of the flow was in the opposite direction. They made good time.

At the airport Peter parked the car and went in with them to the Air Fiji desk, where they checked in for their flight. McCann was surprised to find himself standing on a scale to be weighed with his bag, commenting that he hoped they didn't charge by the kilo for passengers. After the check-in they went to the small food stand, where the Americans had coffee and rolls. Tukana opted for tea and a sandwich.

They chatted as they sipped their drinks, and Tukana told them he was going to be met by a local police officer that he knew in Savusavu to follow up on the tattoos. Maybe he could get a lead on the tribe to which the men murdered in Seattle belonged. They would discuss Mac's cover on the flight.

ELEVEN

Tukana led the way through the gate, and he and McCann walked out to the aircraft. It was a de Havilland DHC Twin Otter, a nineteen seat, high wing turboprop of which Air Fiji had two. They climbed the steps and entered the cabin, Tukana sitting across from the American. There were ten other passengers, so the flight was not full.

The pilot and co-pilot were already aboard and, after all the passengers were seated, the co-pilot went aft and closed the door, drawing in the steps. As he returned to the cockpit, he checked that seat belts had been fastened throughout the cabin.

McCann had not seen the South Pacific from the air before, as he had arrived at night. He was intrigued with the scene below him now. The sunshine was brilliant and sparkled on the ocean, which had many-toned colors of blue and green. There were small islets with differing shades of greenery in the grass and trees, and with sandy beaches which appeared white in some and yellow or brown in others. Surrounding the islands were the reefs, with the coral heads generating another palette of whites, greens and blues.

As they gained altitude, the colors lost their intensity and McCann's interest was drawn back inside the cabin. Tukana was reading the *Fiji Times* and they hadn't spoken since takeoff.

"Is this local cop in Savusavu a friend of yours or just a working acquaintance?" asked McCann.

The Fijian looked up from his newspaper. "We're not close friends like Pete and I are, but I've known him for a lot of years. I like him and trust him. But I wouldn't expect him to keep quiet if we find anything. Does that answer your question?"

"I guess so," answered McCann. "I'm just trying to get a feel for the situation before we get there is all. Is he an expert on the local villages around Savusavu?"

"As much as anybody can be an expert on any area in Fiji," Tukana said. "What we hope for is that he'll take us to someone, who might know someone who might give us the right lead to a couple of missing guys, who just might be identifiable using your pictures of corpses and tattoos."

"You sure make it sound like a long shot."

"That it is, that it is," repeated Tukana, smiling. "But I now realize that the situation in Seattle is deadly serious and that it may pose a threat to thousands of people. If there is a Fiji connection to this thing, then I'll do my best to help you find it. I've spent several hours on the computer since I last saw you. I just wish I could figure out why they need to involve Fiji in their activities."

"Dan, I know you were resentful when Pete first brought us together. I really am glad that you now understand what I'm trying to do here. I believe that there's a group of bad guys here who are working with the terrorists in the Northwest. The local ones may be on to me already, but I haven't seen any sign of them as yet. One way or the other, keep your eyes open. I don't want to be responsible for anything happening to you or Peter."

Tukana looked at the sea far below them. "Why the Fiji connection? What do they need from here?" he mused.

McCann said, "If I knew the answer to that, I'd have a better idea about how to proceed and who to go after. But one thing's for sure—it has to point towards Islamic extremists. Whether or not they're Fiji citizens or foreigners hiding amongst the locals is another question."

The Twin Otter curved in for its landing and taxied across to the terminal. The co-pilot walked aft to open the door and lower the steps, allowing the passengers to disembark.

Tukana led the way, and McCann followed him into the terminal building. As they entered, a bearded Fijian approached them and shook hands with Tukana. They exchanged a few words of greeting in Fijian, and then Tukana turned to McCann.

"Mac, meet Police Sergeant Samuela Cakau." He pronounced the name as "Thakau."

"Sam, this is Gerry McCann, who's visiting from America. Mac is on holiday and is staying with my friend Peter Barclay at Pacific Harbour. He's a mystery writer in Seattle and I invited him to make this trip with me to see a bit more of Fiji and learn how we work here."

Cakau and McCann shook hands.

The new arrivals picked up their bags, and the three men headed for the parking lot and a Toyota sedan. The two Fijians got in the front, and McCann climbed in the back.

"What do you want to do first, Dan?" asked Cakau. "I'm all yours today, and I'm to help you any way I can."

Tukana fished out the postmortem photos that McCann had given him. "These two men were killed in America and are thought to be from Fiji. Ever seen them before?"

Cakau studied the photos for a few moments with a sour look on his face.

"No. Are they supposed to be from here?"

"It's possible they might be." Tukana handed over the tattoo pictures, and Cakau looked them over. "These tattoos were on the victims. Someone on Beqa thought they were similar to tattoos from the Savusavu region and suggested I try here." Cakau handed back the pictures and started the engine.

"I'd like to get started right away, Sam, so I suppose we should head for Dromoninuku village. Do you know anyone there who might be helpful?"

"As a matter of fact, I do," answered the Savusavu cop as he eased the Toyota out of the parking place. "My cousin is from there. He's the schoolteacher in the village. If anybody knows the locals, it's him. If he doesn't know the tattoos, maybe he knows someone who does."

"Let's go see him," urged Tukana, and the small car moved out of the airport.

They drove to Savusavu first and went up to the Hot Springs Hotel that overlooks the beautiful Savusavu Bay with the harbor stretching out to Nawi Island. Tukana checked in, securing rooms for McCann and himself.

They got back in the car to go to lunch. Cakau headed down the hill to Savusavu's one street that ran along the waterfront. He parked at the Copra Shed and they entered the Captain's Café, where they sat outdoors under the shade of a large umbrella.

They each had a beer while they waited for their food. The restaurant began to fill with customers, people who were obviously local, the usual mixture of Fijians, Indians and Europeans. In addition, quite a few tourists were present, most off an air-conditioned coach that had brought them on a tour from Labasa.

The fish and chips were excellent. When McCann was finished, he pushed his chair back a bit from the table and looked around the deck and inside the restaurant. He did not expect to recognize anyone, but seated in a corner of the dining room there was an individual who certainly recognized McCann.

It was the swarthy-appearing man who had been on the flight with him from Seattle to Nadi. He was at a small table with another dark man who was of similar appearance.

The two fitted in with the local Fiji Indian people. They would have been noticeable to the locals only if their conversation was overheard, as they were talking quietly in Urdu, the Muslim language of Pakistan, and not in Hindi that is the language common to Fiji Indians.

The man who had followed McCann on the Air Pacific flight was called Jawad Saliheen. He had been living in the Seattle area for several months. His companion went by the name of Ahmed Aziz, and he had been in Fiji for some weeks, arriving through Australia. Both were members of the Islamic World Federation.

Saliheen murmured quietly, "According to my source from the Suva police office, they're headed for the village of Dromoninuku to look for information on the two Fijians we had to dispose of in Seattle. We can't take any chances on their finding any leads to our activities here. We are getting too close to the next stage of our campaign to take any chances."

Aziz turned to glance out to the deck area. "They will soon be ready to leave. I should go out and take care of things now while you pay the bill." Saliheen nodded, and the other man left the table.

Out in the parking area, he strolled towards Cakau's Toyota that had been left with the windows open because of the heat. Looking around to make sure that he was unobserved, he quickly opened the front passenger door to place a small transmitter under the dash. He then walked casually to a white Mazda sedan parked nearby and got in the driver's seat to await his partner. The other man soon came out and joined him in the car. He took out a newspaper, which partially shielded him as he pretended to read.

McCann, Tukana and Cakau came out of the restaurant shortly afterwards and got into the Toyota. In his car, Aziz turned on the amplifier and increased the volume. They were pleased to hear the doors slamming and the sound of the engine being started in the other car. Cakau backed out and turned the car to head in the direction of Dromoninuku village. They were followed by the men in the Mazda, who were monitoring the detectives' conversation.

The Toyota proceeded along the coast, and when they reached Dromoninuku village, Cakau turned in and parked. The three got out and walked past the bures, nodding and waving to the people and exchanging greetings. Eventually they came to the school that was near the church. Cakau left the other two standing in the shade of a pandanus tree while he went into the school building to find his cousin. After a while he came out with a tall Fijian who had dark bushy hair and wore a sulu and a long-sleeved white shirt. They walked over to join McCann and Tukana under the tree.

"This is my cousin, Bose Nasali. He's the schoolteacher in the village. Bose, meet Dan Tukana, who is a police detective from Suva, and Gerry McCann, who is his friend visiting from America." The men shook hands as all said "Bula."

"Bose, we were hoping you could help us with some inquiries we're making about a couple of murder victims in America," continued Cakau. "There's some suggestion that perhaps they might have come from this area of Fiji."

Tukana handed over the photographs of the two dead men and Nasali looked at them with distaste. Then he raised his eyebrows and wrinkled his brow.

"They look a bit familiar. There were a couple of young fellas here who were in trouble with the village people for bad behavior, and later with the local authorities for burglary and break-ins and those kinds of things. It was about two years ago when they took off from here—probably went to Suva, I suppose."

"Do you remember their names?" asked Tukana.

"No, I didn't actually know them. They weren't from this village, but must have lived nearby."

Tukana handed him the other set of pictures. "How about these tattoos? Do they mean anything to you? Are they a local style?"

The schoolteacher looked over the second bunch of pictures. "These also look familiar, but I'm no expert on tattoo art. The best one to ask here would be old Joe Tau, who probably knows as much as anybody around here about that kind of thing. He lives in that bure over there beyond the church." He pointed to a tin roofed, concrete-block house. "It's the one with the blue curtains."

They thanked Bose Nasali, who turned to get back to his charges. There had been an increasing chatter in the school as the men were outside, and this was cut off suddenly as the teacher reentered.

Cakau asked McCann and Tukana to wait for him and left to return to the car. He was back in a few minutes and McCann smiled when he saw the yagona in his hand—the customary and, no doubt, expected gift.

The three cops walked past the church to the bure. Cakau mounted the two steps to the open door, knocked on the doorpost and called, "Hello. I'd like to speak to Joe Tau. Are you here, Joe?"

There were sounds of someone moving inside and a voice answered, "This is Joe. Who is it?"

Cakau put his head inside and said, "I'm called Samuela Cakau. I'm a police sergeant from Savusavu, and I'm out here with a couple of friends who need your help with some information. My cousin is the schoolteacher, Bose Nasali, and he thought maybe you were the man to talk to."

There was a pause and the sound of grunting. An old man appeared at the door and looked at the three strangers, who all said, "Bula." He nodded and sat down on the top step, his back against the doorpost. Cakau handed him the package of yagona, and the old man said, *Vinaka, vinaka.*"

Tukana stepped forward, presenting the photos of the dead men. "We need to know who these men are. Have you ever seen them?"

From his shirt pocket Tau fished out a pair of wire rimmed reading glasses that had only one earpiece. He set them over his nose and then held up the pictures, looking at them one at a time.

"These men are dead?" he asked.

Tukana answered, "Yes. Did you know them?"

"These men were no good. They were bad men when they lived around here, but I did not know their names."

When he was shown the shots of the tattoos, the old villager recognized the pattern and told them that it belonged to an ancient Fijian tribe who were notorious in history for their viciousness even at a time when all Fijians were cannibals. In recent years this tattoo had been adopted by a modern gang as their logo. He informed them this group had no affiliation with Fiji culture and included members of varying racial background.

"They call themselves the 'Liga Ca,' which means 'Hand of Evil,'" he finished.

There was no more to be learned from Joe Tau and they took their leave after shaking hands with him and thanking him for his help. He sat watching them as they walked back towards the car.

As they drove away from Dromoninuku village they talked about what they had learned there and Saliheen and Aziz in the pursuing car heard the discussion.

Saliheen uttered an oath in Urdu when he found they had learned about the Liga Ca.

"This is bad," he said to Aziz. "We must deal with these infidels. They're getting too close, and this is not the time to have them breathing down our necks when we have so much about to happen here."

Tukana had Cakau drive back to Savusavu, and there they parked the car in the middle of the town. They walked along the street and started the policeman's footslogging routine, going from store to store and into restaurants to show their photographs and ask questions while McCann waited in a cafe. People mostly shook their heads and denied knowing the victims. They had reached the end of town in one direction and were halfway back along the other side of the street when they entered a small marine engine repair place and found a man who nodded when he was shown the pictures.

"I recognize one of them," he said. "He used to hang around here a couple of years ago. I think his name was Satala, but I don't remember his first name."

"What about the other one?" asked Tukana.

"He might have been the guy who ran with Satala, but I don't know for sure and I don't know his name," he answered and then added, "They were bad men."

Learning no more from the man, they thanked him and left.

They gave up on the day's questioning. Cakau picked up McCann and drove him and Tukana back to the Hot Springs Hotel, arranging to pick them up again the next morning.

McCann and Tukana went to their rooms, where they showered and changed. Then they headed down to the bar that was not yet busy.

McCann ordered a double vodka on the rocks, and Tukana had a beer. They sat at the bar, but when the drinks were served they took them outside to a table overlooking the pool. Only a few people were in the water, and most of the action was from a couple of kids at the shallow end.

"We'll take the morning flight back to Nausori," said Tukana. "There's not much point in trying to find out any more around here. I'll put out the word on the Suva underground network to try to get a lead on Satala and the other guy. There should be somebody who knew them and might be able to tell us who they ran with."

TWELVE

Peter opened a bottle of one of his favorite wines, a Cabernet from the Barossa valley in South Australia. He poured a glass and left the wine to breathe as he started to prepare dinner.

He liked to make sauces and now took out some of his favorite ingredients—mayonnaise, Italian dressing, lemon, Dijon mustard, garlic and a Fijian pepper sauce. He sipped on the wine as he readied the items and mixed them together as a marinade for the fish. When he had the mixture to his satisfaction, with frequent tasting between sips of wine, he poured some over the fish and set it aside. Taking a large New Zealand potato from the vegetable bin, he placed it in the microwave oven and set the timer.

He put the marinated mahimahi in the oven and poured another glass of cabernet. He laid a place for himself at the counter and set out butter and condiments. When all was ready, he served the food and thoroughly enjoyed it. The fish was excellent, as was the potato with lashings of butter and a little papaya on the side. After he had finished eating and cleared things away, it was time to leave to pick up Ann Eaton.

The 4Runner made the trip to Nadi in good time to meet the Air Pacific flight, and Peter had coffee at the snack bar while he waited for the passengers to exit from the customs hall.

He had printed "Ms. Eaton" on a card that he could hold up when a likely looking unaccompanied female emerged. He was surprised that there were so many possibilities as he was raising the card for the fourth time before he got a response.

Ann Eaton, dressed in a green blouse and skirt, was no disappointment in her attractive appearance as she came out and stopped to look around the people gathered at the gate. She saw his sign and approached him with a smile, pushing a luggage cart containing two suitcases and her carry-on bag and purse. There was also a sack of duty-free purchases.

"I'm Ann Eaton," she said extending her hand.

"Hi, I'm Dr. Barclay—Peter, that is. Gerry McCann is staying at my place. He asked me to pick you up."

"Thank you for meeting me."

She turned to look over her shoulder. "I see a bank over there. Do I have time to get some Fijian cash?"

"Sure, and that's a good idea as there's no bank in Pacific Harbour where you're going. Why don't you go ahead and I'll take care of your baggage. I'll stow it in the car and come back to get you. You'll be in line for a while."

She took her purse and went to get in line for the bank. Peter pushed the cart out through the door and along to the car. He loaded the suitcases, duty-free sack and carry-on bag in the back and locked the tailgate door. He went back inside and waited for her to come out of the bank. They walked together out to the 4Runner. She did not make the usual American's mistake of heading for the wrong side.

As they started out from the airport he said, "It'll take us a couple of hours plus to Pacific Harbour. Do you need something to eat?"

"No thanks, they fed us very well on the flight. I just need to get to where I'm going and have a shower and a drink and not necessarily in that order. Did McCann book me in somewhere?"

"As a matter of fact, he did," replied Peter. "You're booked into my villa."

She was silent for a moment. "That's very nice, but I wouldn't want to put you to any trouble. You've already got one cop staying with you. You don't need the FBI moving in as well."

"The fact is, you won't be any trouble at all. More importantly, McCann thinks that you need a cover. It seems you're joining your gentleman friend, Gerry McCann, who is on vacation and visiting his old friend from Seattle, Doctor Peter Barclay. How does that sound?"

Ann was quiet as the car continued along the road that bypassed Nadi. She finally answered. "After the airport action in Seattle, with John Kerrigan getting killed and the execution of their own man by those bastards, I believe they would stop at nothing. If McCann figures we need a cover here, then I'll go along with it. It's too bad you have to be involved, though. These people are bad, and if we are in danger, then you are as well."

"If they're on to McCann then I'm already on their list. There's one thing you should understand though. With McCann over in Savusavu and not returning till morning it's just you and me in the villa tonight. Hope that doesn't bother you too much."

"I'm sure you're quite the gentleman."

Peter put a CD in the car's player. Soon Cleo Lane and Mel Torme were entertaining in their inimitable style.

"Hope you like this kind of music," said Peter. "I'm sort of a mainstream jazz fan myself."

"Sounds nice," she responded. "I like most kinds of music except for the hard rock stuff."

They chatted for a while, but by the time they had reached Sigatoka she was leaning against the corner of the seat and appeared to be asleep from then on until they were approaching Deuba.

Shortly afterwards they passed over the bridge and turned into the Pacific Harbour "A" section. Ann was looking at the moonlit trees and hedges on either side as they came to Peter's driveway. As he turned in and drove up to stop at the front door of the villa, they were greeted exuberantly by Koli, much to her delight.

She looked around at the trees and hedges, saying, "The colors must be wonderful in daytime."

"They are," he answered, turning to unload her baggage and then open the door.

They went in, and he led the way to the guest suite next to his office. He deposited the suitcases on the twin bed next to the wall, assuming she would prefer to sleep in the one by the windows.

"Would you like that drink now?" he asked. "You could start on one while you shower."

"That sounds just great," she replied. "Do you have a beer?"

"Do I've a beer!" he said as he went out the door.

He went to the refrigerator and poured a Fiji Bitter into an iced glass from the freezer. Returning to her room, he knocked on the door, and she told him to come in. She was starting to unpack some of her things. She accepted the cold beer and took a sip.

"That tastes great," she said. "I'll shower and be with you in a few minutes."

Peter went back to the kitchen and took out some New Zealand blue cheese, cheddar cheese and several fruits. He placed these on the bar with knives, forks and plates and added bread, butter and crackers.

He put on some soft piano music and opened a beer for himself. He sat at the bar on the kitchen side and was reading the *Fiji Times* when she came through from her side of the villa and climbed onto the stool facing him.

"I thought you might like a snack," he said as she settled herself on the barstool, "or perhaps you're hungrier now and would like me to cook you something?"

"This looks great," she answered, and she cut some blue cheese and took a slice of papaya.

"What would you like to drink? I've a New Zealand white that goes well with that cheese."

"Beer's fine for right now, thanks."

He poured her another Fiji Bitter, opening a second for himself. Sitting down again, he put some cheese and crackers on his plate.

"Where's McCann?"

"He's been trying to find out about the two guys who had their throats cut in Seattle," said Peter. "I introduced him to a friend of mine, Dan Tukana, who's a detective in Suva. They're working together. Up to this point there's no official contact with the Fiji Police, and my friend is quietly trying to find out the identity of the victims.

"Mac and I also made a trip to see another old friend on Beqa, the island across the lagoon from here. We showed him the postmortem pictures from Seattle. He didn't recognize the victims' faces, but thought the tattoos maybe came from the Savusavu region."

"Which is where Mac is?"

"Right. So Mac and my detective friend flew over there this morning." He paused, looking at his watch, "—or rather yesterday morning. Mac called in the evening to say that they found out very little. The dead men did come from the general region over there, and one of them was probably named Satala. Apparently Tukana figures they won't learn any more over there and wants to pursue things in Suva. They're returning in the morning, and I said I'd pick them up at the Nausori airport when they get in."

"And what time is that?"

"The flight is due in at ten-fifteen, so I should leave here about eight-thirty or so. The traffic can be rough at that time."

"Will I be going with you?" she asked.

"I don't know if that would be a good idea. Tukana hasn't been told about your coming here. He might not be too pleased if he knew that the FBI was becoming involved in this when the Fiji authorities haven't been consulted. And I don't want to make any decisions that McCann should make."

He paused and thought a moment before continuing.

"Why don't I drop you off in Suva? You can look around the city while I go on to Nausori and pick them up. After I drop off Tukana at his office, McCann and I will meet you for lunch. Then the two of you can make a decision with regard to telling Tukana about the FBI. It would only be putting things off, but at least that way we could discuss our options."

Ann sat drinking her beer before answering. Then she said, "Okay. Let's do that. I don't want to embarrass either of you, and maybe there's some way to sort things out without compromising anyone."

"Right," agreed Peter. "Now why don't you go get some sleep? You may find yourself waking up early here."

She finished her snack and washed it down with the rest of her beer. She smiled and said goodnight.

He looked after her as she walked towards her bedroom.

THIRTEEN

Ann slept well for five hours or so until the birds awakened her just before dawn. She looked outside. The pool looked so inviting that she donned a swimsuit and headed towards the patio. As she walked through the living room Mere greeted her. "Good morning, miss. I am Mere, Doctor Peter's housegirl."

"How do you do, Mere," said Ann with a smile.

"Would you like some juice? Some coffee or tea perhaps?"

"Juice and a cup of coffee would be very nice, thank you. I'm just going to have a quick swim to help me wake up."

She continued through the living room and out to the patio. Dropping her towel on a chair, she walked down the steps into the pool. She had done four laps when Peter appeared with a cup of coffee in his hand.

"Good morning," he said. "Did you sleep well?"

"Yes, thank you. I slept very well until the birds woke me. You do have quite a few around here."

"You might say that," Peter said with a laugh. "But it's a more pleasant way to wake up than by the noise of traffic outside your window."

Mere came out and asked if they would like to have breakfast. They settled for cereal and fruit with coffee and toast. Ann went off to get dressed while it was being served on the patio. Peter sat down to read the *Fiji Times*.

After they had eaten, it was time to leave. They climbed into the 4Runner to head for Suva. It was a fine, sunny morning as they drove through the countryside, Peter pointing out various trees and plants, naming as many as he could. Ann was intrigued with the enormous Bakawai tree, also known locally as the "rain" tree. There were many of these in the stretch between Pacific Harbour and Navua, where they stood like monstrous domed umbrellas for the cattle, some covering areas as large as tennis courts.

They drove into the city, and he showed her the public market and pointed out the best shopping streets. Eventually he stopped by a public parking lot. He pointed over her shoulder, indicating a restaurant behind the car park.

"That's Cardo's Chargrill and Bar. We'll meet you there at about noon. If all goes according to plan, that should give us time to drop off Tukana back at his office. The restaurant's upstairs. Just grab a table if you get there before us. It shouldn't be too crowded at lunchtime. It's more popular as a dinner place."

"Okay, I'll look around town."

She opened the door and stepped down onto the pavement. He waved to her and drove around the lot to get back on the street that would lead out of town in the direction of Nausori.

Peter had an uneventful trip to the airport and was there before the Savusavu flight was due. The de Havilland landed some ten minutes late. He watched it taxi in to park near the terminal. The engine whine toned down and the propellers came to a stop as the door opened and the steps were lowered.

The passengers emerged and soon McCann came out, followed by Tukana. Peter stepped forward to shake hands with them when they reached the arrivals gate. Peter was amused that McCann was now saying "Bula" like a native.

The two cops grabbed their bags off the luggage cart and they all went out to the parking lot.

"Did you guys have a good trip?" asked Peter as they drove out of the airport.

"Everything was fine," McCann said.

"What exactly did you learn over there?"

Tukana looked at McCann and answered only when he nodded. "We found out that the two Seattle victims were from the Savusavu region and that one was probably called Satala. We had no guesses from anybody on the identity of the other one."

McCann spoke up from the back. "The only other info was that the tattoos connect with a sect called the Liga Ca. That means 'Hand of Evil.'"

"Have you heard of them, Dan? This Liga Ca?" Peter asked, turning to Tukana.

"I've heard of them. But as far as I know they haven't been into much above the petty crime level—burglaries, muggings and that kind of thing. But they're available if somebody had need of a bunch of thugs. They're a mixed lot with no particular racial or religious affiliation. Just give them the money and they'll do whatever you want."

The 4Runner was now proceeding down a fairly steep hill and Peter applied the brakes as they came to a turn at the bottom. As they rounded the bend there was a "crack," and suddenly the car was sliding across the road out of control and heading for the ditch on the other side. The front of the vehicle was shuddering as Peter fought to try to regain control, turning the steering wheel one way and then the other as he tried to follow the direction of the skidding front end.

Several cars were coming the other way, but missed the crashing SUV. Peter almost managed to hold the car on the road, then it swung around and the right back wheel slid over the edge of the ditch. The vehicle tipped over, somersaulted and then rolled down the slope by the side of the road. It finally came to rest on its roof at the bottom of a shallow ravine.

Several cars had stopped by the side of the road above the site of the overturned Toyota. A half dozen people climbed down the slope and gathered around the wrecked vehicle, wrenching at the doors.

Peter groaned when he tried to move because of pain in his right upper arm and shoulder. Two men managed to get the driver's door open and helped him out. He stood by the side of the car looking in at Tukana and McCann, neither of whom appeared to be moving.

The same two men who had gotten him out were working at getting the back door open next to McCann. They failed. Another rescuer eventually opened the other back door and leaned across to McCann's inert form. Peter was relieved to hear him say that he appeared to be breathing.

Tukana was lying against the front passenger door and had severe lacerations across his face. Peter went around to the other side to help as the two unconscious passengers were brought out and laid on the ground by the side of the 4Runner. He made a cursory examination of both and confirmed they were both alive. As he checked Tukana, the Fijian detective started to move around and then groaned as someone tried to wipe the blood from his face with a towel. McCann remained unconscious and showed no signs of response. He had a large bruise on the back of his head.

One of the passengers from a car up on the road had already called for an ambulance on his cell-phone and said that it should be arriving shortly.

McCann and Tukana were made as comfortable as possible with what was available, but Peter did not want them moved until the ambulance arrived with stretchers and other equipment. He pressed towels onto Tukana's wounds to try to staunch the bleeding. Then he handed this task over to one of the rescuers while he went to look at his car.

His main interest was in the front tires, and he found one still inflated. The other tire was shredded, but on the outer wall there was a hole that could have been caused by a bullet. He would have to leave it for a police investigation.

When the ambulance arrived, it was accompanied by a police car.

The police officers and ambulance attendants came down from their vehicles with stretchers and emergency equipment. Peter ignored the police at first as he watched the medics dealing with the unconscious McCann and the semi-conscious Tukana. The policemen recognized Tukana. Peter gave them McCann's name and his own as he continued to watch the medics working on his friends.

Both men were then placed on stretchers with the help of the policemen and some of those who had been first on the scene. They were then carried up the slope to the ambulance.

Peter had one of the policemen retrieve the baggage and some other valuables from the 4Runner. Then he got in the back of the ambulance with McCann and Tukana and two medics after agreeing to talk to the police at the hospital. The pain in his arm and shoulder continued and, as the ambulance moved away from the accident site, one of the medics applied a sling to support the arm. This did little to alleviate the pain, but he refused medication until he reached the hospital.

Peter knew they would be taken to the Colonial War Memorial Hospital, known in Fiji as the C.W.M.H. It is the largest and best equipped facility in the islands, and he knew several of the staff there.

As they drove along he remembered about Ann Eaton, who would be waiting at Cardo's. He used his cell-phone, which had been retrieved from the wreck, and got through to the restaurant. They got Ann on the line, and he told her of the accident.

"Is everyone all right?" she asked.

"No," answered Peter. "Mac is unconscious and Dan is pretty cut up. We're in the ambulance on the way to the hospital now."

"How about you? Are you okay?"

"I'm not badly hurt, but I have pain in my right arm and shoulder. I probably won't know any more until they X-ray it."

"I'll grab a cab and see you at the hospital," she said.

The ambulance continued to Suva with the siren wailing and eventually entered the hospital grounds, pulling to a halt at the emergency entrance. The door was opened and Peter stepped out, waiting as the stretchers were removed. He followed the group into the emergency room.

Peter didn't recognize the duty doctor. He was efficient and capable as he looked over the accident victims.

Peter wanted a neurologist or neurosurgeon to look at McCann, who still showed no signs of regaining consciousness. For this reason he asked a young woman at the check-in desk to page his friend, Dr. Geoffrey Pasaam. Within minutes the head pathologist returned the call.

"Peter, old friend, what's going on?"

"Hi, Geoff. I've been in an accident with a couple of friends. They're badly hurt. You know Dan Tukana; he has some bad facial cuts. He was unconscious for a while, but is coming around now. The other guy is a friend visiting from Seattle, and he's still not responding. Who's the best man to take a look at him?"

Pasaam wasted no time. "I'll get a hold of James Cooligan. He's the best man on head injuries that we have around here."

Peter went back to his friends as he waited. They had given Tukana a shot, and he was no longer groaning. His temporary roadside dressings had been removed, and the ER doctor and a nurse were washing his wounded face. The ER doctor paused to look at Peter as he approached.

"Someone mentioned that you're a doctor. These lacerations on your friend's face warrant better surgical repair than

I can offer, so we're just cleaning him up for now. We'll get a plastic surgeon to see him."

Peter nodded. "That's good, I appreciate your good care."

"What about your shoulder? We'd better have that X-rayed." He turned to another nurse who was walking by and asked her to have Peter taken to the radiology department for stat films of his shoulder and upper arm.

"How's the pain?" asked the doctor. Peter admitted that his shoulder was hurting quite a bit, and he was placed in a wheelchair and given a pain shot before being taken for the X-rays.

As Peter was being wheeled out the door, Geoffrey Pasaam called to say that the head injury specialist was on his way.

FOURTEEN

Peter was studied in the radiology department under the supervision of the head radiologist. It was apparent that Pasaam had exerted his influence to ensure that his friend's care at the C.W.M.H. would be the best.

The X-rays revealed no bone damage. The radiologist had more X-rays taken at different angles and diagnosed a separation of the acromio-clavicular joint. Of course, additional soft tissue injury could not be ruled out, as he had severe bruising and swelling in the upper arm and shoulder. The films were studied by an orthopedic surgeon, who suggested immobilizing the arm until the swelling was reduced. This would also lessen the pain. He explained that A-C joint separation did not usually require surgery. It would be painful, but would gradually get better without intervention.

Pasaam came in as Peter's sling and arm fixation were being applied.

"How's it going, mate?" he said, looking at Peter's wrappings. "Maybe this'll help your golf swing!"

Peter managed a smile. He stood up and, having no nausea or dizziness, decided to leave the wheelchair behind.

Tukana had been taken into surgery to have his facial injuries repaired by a plastic surgeon. This specialist had considerable experience in this field, as Fiji's road accident rate was notoriously high.

McCann remained unconscious and was being studied for brain hemorrhage under the care of the neurosurgeon. Peter guessed they would operate to relieve intracranial pressure if a subdural hematoma was suspected.

By the time he got through with his own care and checking on the others, Ann Eaton had been waiting for almost two hours. Pasaam had taken her to the doctor's lounge, where she would be fairly comfortable as she waited and worried about the three men. He now escorted Peter to the lounge but did not enter with him.

She stood up as Peter came into the room.

"Peter, are you all right? How bad are your injuries?"

"I'll survive," he said. "They tell me that nothing's broken. I've a shoulder separation with bruising and contusions."

"What about the others?"

"Dan is in surgery being stitched up. Mac is still unconscious and is being worked up for possible intracranial hemorrhage. They may have to operate on him too."

They talked about the crash, and Peter told her of his suspicion that someone had shot out a front tire.

"I'll have to get to the American Embassy," Ann said. "Looks like it's time to make my presence here official, and that means checking in with the local U.S. head of mission."

Pasaam stuck his head in the door at that moment. "Hate to bring up more problems, but I'm to let you know that the police are still waiting to talk to you, Pete. They're in the ER waiting room." The door closed behind his announcement.

Peter grimaced again as he turned away from the door. "Okay," he said. "We might as well get it over with. Also, I'll have to talk to Tukana's boss at headquarters. I'll have to explain what happened and what I know about the Savusavu trip."

Ann looked at him with a worried expression. "We're going to lose the cover if you tell him too much. We owe it to Tukana to talk to him first before we let anybody else in on this thing."

"There are others in on it already—the guys who shot out the tire on the car. Remember them?"

"Maybe for now you ought to give a statement suggesting that the car crashed because you swerved to avoid another vehicle or something like that, and leave out anything about the shooting thing," she suggested. "That should give us time to talk to Tukana before we let anyone else know what's going on."

Peter thought about it as his arm continued to throb.

"Okay," he allowed. "I'll try to get away with as little as possible in the police statement. But it might be difficult if they start asking about Mac's involvement in the Savusavu investigation."

Peter went out to the ER waiting room to find the police officers.

They had returned to the hospital about an hour before and were not pleased about having to wait so long to speak to him.

After rechecking his name and address, they asked him about the accident and what caused it. Peter told them he'd swerved to avoid an oncoming car that was taking the bend too wide and was on his side of the road. They had reported Tukana's involvement in the crash and his boss, Chief Inspector Charles Dunham, would be coming to see him when Dan had recovered sufficiently.

The two policemen asked about the other occupant, and Peter informed them that he was a friend visiting from

Seattle. He explained that McCann's home address and other data were at his villa, and he would be contacting people in Seattle when he got home.

Peter laid on the pain and suffering quite a bit, and the policemen told him they would not bother him with any further questioning for now. They would need to talk to him again later.

Peter was relieved to be free of them. He went back to check on the progress of Tukana's surgery and to see what they had decided about McCann.

Tukana was in the recovery room and was still semi-conscious. His procedure had been performed under general anesthesia due to the extensive area to be repaired. The surgeon was quite pleased with the results.

McCann had been diagnosed with a subdural hematoma as predicted and had been taken into surgery already to evacuate the thrombus and relieve the pressure on his brain. This was a relatively simple maneuver consisting of making a burr-hole in the cranium to drain out the clot. After that, it would be a matter of time—waiting to see if he reawakened and, if he did, to assess his residual brain function.

Ann Eaton grabbed a cab outside the hospital and had the driver take her to the American Embassy on Loftus Street. The U.S. did not have an ambassador to Fiji at this time, and the head of mission was a Chargé d'Affairs, Craig Kendall.

On arrival at the embassy she asked to see Mr. Kendall, indicating that she was on official business and that it was urgent. She was asked to wait, and after some time a young lady approached and invited Ann to follow her into her office.

"You don't have an appointment?" she asked as she closed the door behind them. They sat across the desk from each other.

"No, this is an emergency situation, and I need to inform the Head of Station of something which is strictly confidential and very urgent. I cannot discuss this with anyone else. All I can tell you is that I have federal credentials, which I do not carry on my person. Please inform the Chargé d'Affairs what I have told you."

The woman left the room, closing the door behind her, after making it clear by her demeanor that she was displeased with Ann's abrupt tone. After some five minutes, she returned accompanied by an embassy guard in the uniform of the U.S. Marine Corps.

"This man will take you to see the Chargé," she said.

Ann and the guard went to the receptionist's desk outside the office of the Chargé d'Affairs. She was asked to take a seat, and the guard stood beside her as the woman behind the desk picked up a phone and after a moment said, "She's here now," and then, "Yes sir." She replaced the handset and turned back to continue working at her computer.

Minutes later the phone beeped and she answered, "Yes sir," and then again said, "Yes sir."

As she replaced the handset again, she told Ann that Mr. Kendall would see her now. She ushered them through to the office behind her and closed the door after them. The guard remained just inside the door as Ann crossed the room.

As she approached him, the Chargé d'Affairs stood and extended his hand. "I am Craig Kendall," he said as they shook hands.

She did not give her name in return, but instead handed him her card identifying her as a special agent of the FBI saying, "Mr. Kendall, what I've to discuss with you is highly confidential at this time and I need to see you alone."

Kendall looked at her identification card and then back at Ann for a few moments before turning to the guard. "All right, sergeant. Please wait in the outer office." The guard went out, closing the door behind him.

Kendall gestured with an open hand towards a visitor's chair. After Ann sat down, he resumed his own seat.

"Well, Special Agent Eaton, what is this all about, and why is there an FBI presence in Fiji? I've not been informed of such by the State Department or any other government agency."

Ann knew she was going to have a hard time explaining her presence and that of McCann in Fiji without the knowledge and approval of the Fijian government, or at least of one of the local security agencies.

For the next thirty to forty minutes, she told him of the bomb threat and murders in Seattle and of the Seatac airport action with the killing of John Kerrigan by the terrorists. Kendall recalled hearing of these events, but did not interrupt her.

She told him about Peter, and he remembered meeting him on the golf course and at some embassy function. She did not dwell upon McCann's trip to Fiji, simply saying he was a friend of Peter's and was a member of the Seattle PD. She explained that a Fijian detective friend of Peter's had taken him on a trip to Savusavu.

Lastly she told him of the car crash and the severe injuries to McCann and Tukana.

"Now, as I understand it," said Kendall, "McCann undertook his trip on his own initiative, whereas you were sent here by your Seattle FBI Chief Agent?"

"Yes sir."

"Then how come I was not informed of your presence until now? How am I supposed to explain an FBI agent being in Fiji without an official invitation or prior arrangement?"

"Sir, we were attempting to keep the investigation covert. We're trying to find out about the Fiji connection to the terrorists in Seattle, and perhaps that might give us a lead as to what their plans are. They appear set on causing massive destruction and loss of life somewhere in the Northwest."

"And what do you want me to do?" he asked.

"McCann will be in the hospital for quite some time if he survives, and I think it would be best if you didn't let it be known that he's a cop—just that he's an American from Seattle who was in an auto accident while visiting his old friend,

Peter Barclay, a retired doctor who lives at Pacific Harbour. That's McCann's cover, and I'm supposed to be his girlfriend joining him on holiday.

"There's one other thing you should know," she continued. "Peter Barclay does not believe the car crash was an accident. Just before the car ran out of control, he heard what he thinks was a shot. He managed a quick look at the front tire and found what he thinks may be a bullet hole. That wheel needs looking at. Maybe we could arrange for the car to be brought in and inspected. Tukana would have done that, but he's in no shape to deal with it right now."

"The Fiji police should be dealing with it," Kendall said.

"And if we let them know about the shot, then we lose our cover and a possible advantage over the terrorists," she said, her anger rising. "Right now they think that they haven't been suspected and can carry on with impunity. It's a game we play sometimes to let them go far enough to hang themselves."

Kendall stood up and looked out the window. This was not a game to him. But Ann Eaton had convinced him of the horrendous consequences of losing.

"It seems to me that we have to continue with a Fiji police presence in this thing," he said. "Now that Tukana is out of action, we have to find another way to approach them."

Ann was worried the whole thing would get out of hand if too many people were let in on the investigation in Fiji. She now said so.

She finished by asking, "Isn't there someone you know in the Fiji security system who can get us the cooperation we need while still keeping things confidential? There must be somebody with that kind of security who would understand the terrible outcome should we fail to stop these terrorists."

Kendall went back to one of his long pauses.

"I'll just have to have a conference with someone fairly high up in the Fiji Police Force. I have a pretty good relationship with the director of the CID, Ilisoni Kabuta. Every now and then we have to arrange for the embassy to be guarded when there are global anti-American threats issued by some of our terrorist friends." He paused again.

"But no matter whom we talk to, they're not going to be pleased that we've had U.S. police and FBI personnel here without their knowledge. I'll call Kabuta right now and see if he can see us immediately. We can't let this thing wait."

"Mr. Kendall," added Ann. "We should consider Dr. Barclay as 'involved,' if only tangentially. He does know more than both of us would like."

Kendall nodded. "Why don't you wait outside for a few minutes while I make the call."

"While you're doing that, may I make a call on a secure line to the U.S.? I need to make a report to my boss in Seattle."

Kendall called out to his secretary and told her to arrange the call for Special Agent Eaton from a private office. Ann left Kendall's office and was escorted to another office where, the secretary picked up the phone and punched in some numbers. She then handed over the receiver to Ann. "Just enter the local area code and number and you'll be connected on a secure line."

After the woman left Ann punched in the 206 Seattle prefix and then George Paxton's direct number. It was answered right away.

"Yes," said Paxton's voice abruptly.

"This is Eaton," she said. "I'm calling from the American Embassy in Suva."

"Well, well. Agent Eaton. How are you, and are you enjoying your vacation, Ann?"

"I'm fine, sir, but there's been some action here with a car crash involving McCann, Doctor Barclay and the Fijian cop they were working with. McCann is still unconscious, and the other two were also injured but are okay."

She went on to tell him what she knew of the events to date, including Peter's suggestion that the tire had been shot out to cause the crash.

Paxton questioned her for a while, and she told him that the Chargé d'Affairs was arranging for them to see the Fijian CID Director.

"I don't know that that's the best way to go," he said. "But I've no other ideas about what to do at this stage. I guess we'll just have to go along with it. Call me again after the meeting with the CID."

"I'll do that, Chief, but it may be best to send you an e-mail when we get to Barclay's place later. I don't trust the phone service down here."

After a pause, Paxton added, "I've to point out that you should keep a low profile. You're going to have to take a back seat and not be too pushy with the Fijians in charge. There are international issues involved now."

"Yes sir." She returned to the Chargé's outer office to wait for Kendall.

FIFTEEN

The 4Runner was taken care of by Peter. He had called upon the old friend who had looked after the car since he had bought it, and arranged for him to take out a wrecker and bring it in to his garage and repair shop. The vehicle was a write-off, but he wanted to have it inspected—especially the punctured front tire. He told his mechanic friend to let nobody near the car until they had gone over it together.

McCann had had his subdural hematoma surgery and was being closely monitored. He was showing some response to stimulation, and his coma appeared to be lightening. With some luck he might be awakening. But the chance of complete recovery was still in doubt.

Peter also got to see Tukana, who was now fully awake. His face and head were swathed in dressings with only one eye, his mouth and his ears uncovered. He could talk only with difficulty due to the bandages. Conversation was painful.

Peter explained what he knew of the crash and ensuing events. He told him of his belief that the front tire had been shot out, and Tukana said that he too remembered hearing the noise of a possible shot. Peter told him about having his friend deal with the wrecked car and said he would give him a follow-up after he had inspected it. Tukana agreed it was a good idea to keep this quiet for now.

Peter was worried about his further interrogation by the police but his concern was lessened when Ann Eaton came through on his cell-phone.

"Peter, I'm just leaving the Embassy," she said. "I've had a long talk with the Chargé. He was very upset at first, but he now seems to understand the situation pretty well. He's called the head of the Fijian CID, and we're to meet with him at police headquarters."

After a short pause, Peter said, "I tell you what. You must be starving, and I know I am. Grab a cab and meet me at Cardo's. You'll have time."

On the way out Peter stopped to tell Tukana of the meeting with Kabuta arranged by Kendall. Tukana said that Kabuta was a tough cop who would probably not take kindly to the uninvited American police activity in Fiji. He also said that he expected to be severely censured by Kabuta for cooperating with McCann without official approval.

Ann was already at the restaurant when Peter arrived. She had ordered a draft beer for him, and it was served as he sat down at the table.

He looked at her and asked, "How are you holding up?"

"Probably better than you are," she responded with a smile.

"How did the meeting go with the Chargé? He must have been annoyed with you and McCann, not to mention the FBI and the Seattle Police Department."

"He was pissed, to say the least," she said. "No doubt he's been on the horn to FBI Headquarters and the State

Department since I left him. I just hope he doesn't blow the whole thing into the open."

"He wouldn't be that stupid," said Peter.

"Not intentionally," she said, sipping her beer. "But it's hard to keep this sort of thing quiet if too many people know about it."

"Anyhow," Peter added, "the next meeting, the one with Kabuta, will decide the future of the investigation in Fiji. If he cooperates, you should be able to continue with the blessing of the Fiji CID. If not, it may be finished."

She nodded. "I'm hoping that, if Kabuta does go along with us, I'll be able to keep Tukana out of trouble."

After a pause, she added, "Well, we'll see what happens," smiling and lightening the mood. "Now, what are we going to have to eat? You were right, I am starving."

The CID Headquarters was nearby in Vanua House and they left the restaurant about fifteen minutes before the appointed meeting with Kendall and Kabuta. The cab dropped Ann off before taking Peter on to the hospital.

"Good luck, Ann," he said as she got out.

"This is my job," she answered. "I'll join you later."

She was in the waiting room for no more than five minutes when Kendall arrived.

"This is a very complicated situation," he said as he sat down to wait with her. Ann did not respond.

The young Indian woman sitting at the reception desk answered her phone and then nodded. "The director will see you now," she said quietly. She opened the door to the inner office, holding it as they entered.

Kabuta rose from his desk. He was tall with a heavy build, and had a large "walrus" mustache on his dark skinned face. He was wearing a long sleeved white shirt with no tie over light blue trousers.

"Mister Kendall," he said, smiling and shaking hands with the Chargé.

Kendall smiled back, and then turned to Ann.

"Mister Kabuta, I'd like to have you meet Miss Ann Eaton of the FBI."

Kabuta shook hands with her, and the two visitors sat down in front of Kabuta's desk as he resumed his seat.

"Mister Director," the Chargé began. "I'm not sure how you wish to open this conference but, if I may make a suggestion, it would appear to me that the best way to begin would be to have Special Agent Eaton present her version of the happenings in Seattle and Fiji as related to this case to date." He paused. "Would this be satisfactory, sir?"

Kabuta sat back in his chair and folded his arms.

"Yes, it would. Proceed, Ms. Eaton."

As she had done in Kendall's office, Ann Eaton described the entire scenario, beginning with the Seattle Police and the murdered Fijians and continuing through the Seatac action and the killing of Kerrigan and the terrorist. She explained what information was hers first hand and what came from Dr. Peter Barclay and his guest, Gerry McCann.

Finally she described the car wreck, including Peter's belief that the tire had probably been shot out to cause the crash.

Kabuta stood up and paced behind his desk.

"This is a mess," he said quietly.

He looked across his desk at them.

"Neither of you is personally responsible for how this thing got started on the wrong foot, but the mismanagement cannot be excused. McCann, Peter Barclay, people in charge, have continued to ignore protocol and abused the relationship of our two countries."

Kendall spoke then. "Mister Director, we know how upset you are at the absence of protocol in this matter, but please consider the horrendous slaughter planned by these terrorists. The various agencies involved had no alternative but to try to maintain secrecy at all costs."

"And just what would you have me do now, Mister Kendall?" Kabuta said. "I can't let American FBI agents and policemen parade around my country doing what they want with no official standing or permission. They've already been abusing privilege by not applying for any permission from us in the first place."

There was a long pause as they sat in strained silence.

Finally Kabuta spoke again.

"You have put me in a very awkward position. On the one hand, I am obliged to observe the necessary protocol regarding police and security force action in my own country. On the other hand, you have spelled out very clearly the great threat to the people in your country." He picked up his pen, slowly rotating it between his thick fingers.

"I am well aware of the evils of terrorism throughout the world and would like to contribute to its demise. Now you're telling me that Fiji has become a possible haven for these people, and I have no alternative but to cooperate in any enterprise directed against them.

"I shall work with you and your people. But this matter shall remain strictly confidential between you and me and the other people directly involved." He carefully put down the pen. "Until it's resolved," he added.

"What you may not like about the arrangement," he went on, "is that I'll be in command of the Fiji operation. I'll expect all concerned to be answerable to me while in Fiji."

Kendall sat up straight in his chair and looked Kabuta straight in the eye.

"Director Kabuta," he said, ""I agree completely. We must keep this investigation under the strictest secrecy. And working through you is acceptable."

They appeared to be finished for now and were surprised when, as they rose to leave, Kabuta resumed.

"I think, Miss Eaton, that you should bring Doctor Barclay with you tomorrow. Normally, we would not condone the involvement of a civilian in an investigation run by the Fiji Police. However, this is a clandestine operation and the usual rules do not necessarily apply here. Besides, I can hardly get in any more trouble if things don't work out. Anyhow, he's already deeply involved and could be of great help to us. Another reason is that we are going to need a number of people and using one who is already in place means one less to recruit. Do you think he would wish to continue to participate, Miss Eaton?"

Ann smiled. "I think you would have a hard time discouraging him, sir."

Kabuta looked at his watch. "That's it for now then. Thank you."

Kendall and Agent Eaton stood. Brief handshakes concluded the meeting.

Once outside, Kendall seemed more relaxed. They got in his car and were driven to the Embassy, where the Chargé got out after telling Ann Eaton to keep him posted on all of the action in the case. He said good-bye and had the driver take her on to the hospital.

Tukana was in good form and greeted Ann politely. She told him of the meeting with Kabuta and the arrangement that the CID Director had demanded. Tukana was surprised they had come out as unscathed as they had, and was glad to know he was still on the team.

"I'm sure I'll still have to go through a pretty bad chewing out when I get out of here," he allowed.

Ann and Peter went to see McCann. He was still semiconscious, but his monitoring showed that he was continuing to make progress. Peter talked to the neurosurgeon before they left and was relieved to learn that hope for a full recovery was now more promising.

They took a cab to Pacific Harbour. To avoid having to cook that evening, Peter decided that they should go to the Oasis Restaurant that was run by his friends Monica Vine and Colin Head. Colin was something of a car buff.

Monica greeted them as they entered, and he introduced her to Ann. "Watch out for this one," said the proprietress with a grin as she greeted her.

They moved over to climb on stools at the bar.

"G'day, Colin," said Peter to the man behind the bar and introduced him to Ann.

"G'day, Doc," he answered. "Heard you wrapped up the 4Runner. Anyone hurt?"

"Yeah. Dan Tukana and a friend of mine got pretty bad injuries, but they seem to be recovering." Then he continued, "Do you have a car I could use?"

"There's a Toyota right outside that you can have. I don't really need it at present."

Peter agreed to rent the car from Colin, and they ordered their meal as they had a drink at the bar. They had an excellent dinner, with curried prawns for Ann and rack of lamb for Peter accompanied by an Australian Syrah.

Ann drove them back to the villa in the gray Toyota.

SIXTEEN

The ferry from Victoria, B.C., approached the dock at Port Angeles, slowed and, bumping off the pilings, settled into her berth at the ferry terminal. The deck hands reached for the mooring lines and secured them to the large cleats. One man pressed a button on the end of the dock extension, and the ramp lowered into position onto the car deck.

After the barricade net was removed from the front of the open bow and the chocks were taken away from the wheels of the foremost vehicles, the cars began to exit the ship and move forward to approach the U.S. Customs check point. Each car was summoned to a customs inspector and moved forward in turn when the light turned from red to green.

The inspectors were quite cursory with most of the passengers, determining the place of residence and country of citizenship of each car's occupants and asking some declaration questions about firearms, alcoholic beverages and tobacco products. Most arrivals were then wished a "pleasant stay" or a "welcome home" and passed through with no further delay.

The customs service was well trained and courteous. They were also very good at their job. Every so often a vehicle would be directed to the side parking area beyond the metered inspection gates and a further examination would take place, which involved a search of the car. If anything unusual was discovered, the car's occupant or occupants would be invited inside for further interrogation—and possibly a body search.

The customs inspection of the vehicles off the Victoria ferry had been proceeding in the usual uneventful fashion when one of the inspectors waved to call on a car stalled in his line. The vehicle finally moved into the inspection bay, and the inspector started the usual routine by asking the driver where he was from. The driver said in a thick accent that he was from Canada. When asked about his nationality, he also answered that he was from Canada. The inspector, now suspicious of the man's demeanor, directed him to the secondary search area. The vehicle then started forward and parked. A customs inspector came to the side of the car and asked the driver to unlock the trunk and get out of the vehicle. The driver did as he was told, but once he was outside the car he suddenly turned around and began running away in the direction of the front of the ferry terminal. The customs inspector yelled and started in pursuit, joined by a policeman on duty at the entrance.

They chased the fugitive for some six blocks as he ran along the street out of the port. He went down First Street, nearly knocking over a couple of people, and then tried to get into a car that had stopped at an intersection. The driver locked the door and drove off.

He ran right onto Lincoln, where the agents and police officers closed in on him. The dark haired man offered no resistance as they led him away. When the fugitive's Canadian rental car was searched, the trunk was found to contain thirty-two ounces of what was thought to be nitroglycerin. There were also other bomb-making materials, including four timers.

George Paxton had no sooner put down his phone after receiving the report from Ann Eaton in Fiji when he got the call from the U.S. Customs Service in Port Angeles. He called Fisher and Molson into his office.

"Customs in Port Angeles just grabbed someone bringing in explosive materials and timers," he told them. "You two better get up there right away and bring him down to the Federal Detention Center at Seatac."

"Is this somebody that we know about?" Fisher asked.

"All we know at the moment is that he's an Algerian who was carrying a phony Canadian passport. They did a good job in nailing him. That stuff could have caused a lot of death if he'd gotten through with it. Call me when you get to Port Angeles. I want to be kept informed of anything you find out about this guy. I'll have to get the Counter-Terrorist Squad together, and I want to keep them up to date on this."

Fisher and Molson grabbed their coats and headed down to the ferry terminal. They used their priority to go to the front of the line and board the waiting boat to Bainbridge Island.

After the forty-minute trip to Bainbridge, they went across the island and the Hood Canal Bridge to the Olympic peninsula with the snow-capped Olympic Mountains ahead. They then drove around the peninsula to Port Angeles and the police headquarters.

After time spent on paper work, they finally loaded the handcuffed Algerian in the back of the car next to Molson. At the Federal Detention Center they handed over their prisoner, who had remained silent, and then they returned to the FBI headquarters in Seattle.

The terrorist was found to have two ferry ticket stubs on him. So it appeared that there was another person involved who may have walked off the boat as a foot passenger and was now missing. They also found a pen bearing the name of a motel in Vancouver, B.C. Investigation by Canadian authorities revealed that he had stayed at that motel under the name of Ressam. Further investigation revealed that Ressam had a reservation for one night at a Seattle motel near the Space Needle and that he had a plane ticket for London the next day.

George Paxton presented all this information to the Special Counter-Terrorist Squad. It was decided that the mayor's office had to be informed, because of possible threat to the city of Seattle, maybe involving the Space Needle in the Seattle Center.

A few days later the squad met again to be updated by Paxton.

"We have several developments," he began. "Firstly, an Abdel Hakim Tizegha was arrested on the east side in Bellevue and charged with illegally entering the United States about a month ago." He paused to consult his notes. "A Brooklyn resident, Abdel Ghani, was arrested by the FBI and was charged with aiding and abetting Ahmed Ressam. There's evidence that Ghani spent a week in Seattle about the time of Ressam's arrest in Port Angeles and that he was here to meet him. Ghani was said to have had several telephone conversations with 'an associate in Seattle' in recent weeks." Paxton paused again. "This concerned using fraudulent credit cards to obtain cash. We think he may have been talking to Tizegha or to another member of their group."

Ron Marsh of the Secret Service spoke then. "What more have we learned about Ressam since we last met?"

"According to Canadian immigration documents, he was accused of arms dealing and belonged to a terrorist group in Algeria. He may have been a fighter in Afghanistan in the war against the Russians too. He arrived in Montreal in 1994 with a fake French passport and said he was seeking exile. While in Montreal he worked as a grocer, but was also an accused thief there. When he failed to show for a hearing that would have prompted his removal from Canada, a warrant was issued for his arrest."

Paxton scanned the faces around the table. "Since we last met, the Mayor was given all we've got on a possible bombing, and this caused him to cancel the big New Year's celebration at Seattle Center. It was the only prudent thing to do.

"We have to remember that Canada's lax immigration laws have led to a bad situation for the U.S. as well as themselves," he went on. "According to Canadian intelligence officers, there are at least fifty known terrorist groups in Canada. Montreal alone has some fifteen thousand Algerian immigrants, and in that city there's a ring of thieves and extortionists who bankroll terrorist groups in Algeria. Strict laws in this country prevent fund raising here by foreign groups.

"Gentlemen, these people are just north of us across the most friendly and, I might add, most poorly policed border in the world. There are less than three hundred agents along the entire U.S.-Canadian border. We have over eight thousand agents along the border between Mexico and us. Yet the extremist groups, who are the biggest threat to us, are north of the border, not south. Up till now they've been killing our people in overseas outposts. Things may be changing. They're making moves on our home soil."

The men around the table had been making notes. When he paused again, Len Williams of the CIA spoke for the first time. "There's been a hunt on for another Algerian-born suspect by the name of Hamid Aich. He moved to Dublin from Canada last June. The Irish police questioned him at the request of the Canadian authorities in December, but since then he's disappeared."

Paxton nodded. "The only other recent matter for us was the arrest of another Algerian or Moroccan by the name of Youssef Karroum at Blaine, WA. He was searched when coming across the border. Traces of nitrates were found in his car and confirmed by bomb-sniffing dogs."

Paxton then began to discuss the latest activities in Fiji. He gave them a synopsis of the report made to him by Agent Eaton by telephone from the U.S. Embassy, and there was a discussion of the car crash and the resulting injuries to McCann and Tukana. In answer to their concerns about McCann, he could only tell them that he'd had surgery to relieve pressure on his brain and was coming slowly out of his coma.

Eaton's e-mail report of the meeting with Kabuta created quite an eruption over a foreigner controlling the action when it involved U.S. federal and police personnel.

"Nothing we can do about it at the moment," Paxton said. "It's on Fijian turf, and we're not even there as far as Washington is concerned."

SEVENTEEN

Peter finally gave up after a night of intermittent sleep and arose at dawn. He went out to the kitchen to put on a pot of coffee. Then he sat by the pool and watched the Fiji morning arrive. Ann Eaton came out at 7:30, dressed and ready for work.

"We should get to Suva early and find out how things are shaping up with Tukana," she said. "If he's up to it, we can sit down with him and try to figure out the best way to sort things out with Kabuta so we can all work together."

"You don't think Kabuta would dismiss him from the investigation at this stage, do you?" Peter asked.

"I don't know. Remember that Kabuta is pretty burned at all of us for pursuing this thing behind the backs of the whole Fijian law enforcement establishment. But he's really upset with Tukana, and that's understandable when you think about it."

They were in Suva about an hour later. They made their way up to the C.W.M.H. When they went looking for Tukana, they found his room empty. A nurse told them she thought he had gone to visit McCann. They went to McCann's room in the intensive care area and found Tukana there by the bed. McCann appeared to be arguing with him and was mumbling to himself at the same time.

"This man is impossible," said Tukana as they approached. "He wants to get out of bed right now and go after the guys who put him there."

"I want out of here, and the sooner the better," McCann said.

"You're going to have to let the doctors decide when you can get up," said Ann.

"And since when do I need orders from the FBI?"

"How are you doing today?" asked Peter, looking at Tukana.

"I'm okay. Ready to get back to work too."

"You see?" broke in McCann. "It's all right for him to get out, but I've to go on lying here."

"It's not all right for either of you to leave without your doctors' approval," said Peter. "I'll talk to them."

Peter found the plastic surgeon scrubbing up for a procedure. He had already seen Tukana that morning and agreed to let him leave the hospital, but on the strict understanding that he would return for inspection of his wounds. Peter thanked him and went to find the neurologist. After waiting at his office for some time, he eventually got to see Dr. Peterson, and they talked about McCann's future care.

"I'm delighted he's recovered his brain function so quickly and with no apparent residual damage," said Peterson. "However, we must be careful we don't rush things. He could easily have another bleed, so we have to keep him quiet for the next several days, even if it means sedating him. We've been treating him for cerebral edema, as that's common with brain injury as I'm sure you know. Now we have to watch his blood pressure."

When Peter Barclay got back to McCann's room, he was greeted with, "Well. What's the word? Do I get out of here or what?"

Peter's response was to say to Tukana and Ann, "Why don't you wait for me outside while I have a few words with Mac."

Peter sat down and faced McCann.

"Mac, you've had a very severe head injury and are most fortunate to have recovered as well as you have. There's no apparent residual brain damage. But you could have another hemorrhage if you get a sudden rise in your blood pressure. It's essential you be kept quiet in bed for several days. Okay?"

"Well, I'm not going to like it. I don't need other people to do my work for me, and that includes all three of you."

"You dumb sonofabitch, we need you on this thing. But we won't have you to help us if you lose what brain you have!"

"All right, Doc, but you're going to have to keep me posted."

"Okay, Mac. We'll keep you informed. Now try to get some sleep, and we'll see you later."

Peter left the room and went to find Tukana and Ann to discuss their next move, which they agreed had to be a meeting with Kabuta. Ann got on her cell-phone and called the CID director. He said he would see them in his office as soon as they got there.

This time there was no waiting when they got to Kabuta's office.

Kabuta's first words were for Tukana. "You're most fortunate, Detective, that you're here and not in jail."

"Sorry, sir."

"How do you feel under those bandages?"

"I've felt better, sir."

Turning to Peter, Kabuta growled, "And I'm not too pleased with your part in this, doctor." Peter looked contrite but said nothing.

There was a pause as Kabuta shuffled some papers around on his desk. "Let's move on. What about McCann?"

"He's alive," Ann said. "He's recuperating in C.W.M.H."

"Very well," said Kabuta. "Now what do you have?"

Tukana spoke up. "The only lead we have is through the Fijians murdered in Seattle. We found someone in Dromoninuku village who connected them with a gang called the Liga Ca, or "Hand of Evil." We questioned people in stores and restaurants in Savusavu and finally found a man who recognized one of the Seattle homicide victims. He told us he thought the dead man was called Satala. We couldn't learn anything else about them except that they were known locally as bad boys. Somebody mentioned they'd left the region, and he thought they had probably gone to Suva."

"So what do you propose, detective?"

"Our first priority should be this Liga Ca gang. This will mean hitting on our informers and snitches."

"Excuse me, sir," Ann said. "But that brings up concern about the confidentiality of this investigation."

Kabuta studied her. "I appreciate your concern, Agent Eaton, but just how do we go about an investigation without involving personnel who know the territory? We need all channels open."

Tukana spoke up again. "Sir, I think I can get a couple of people who'd be discreet without letting the American involvement become known. They're experienced, and I've worked with them before." Kabuta nodded, and Tukana then went on.

"I was thinking that we could use my place in Lami. We have to have a place to meet without attracting attention, and Salote wouldn't mind, I'm sure." He was referring to Salote Turuva, with whom he had been living for several years and was well known to Tukana and Peter.

"Good idea," said Kabuta. "That's settled then." He rose, making it clear the meeting was over.

"Get started on this Liga Ca and the connection with these men murdered in Seattle. Clear this thing up as soon as possible."

After leaving the CID Director's office, they took a cab, Ann and Peter going back to the hospital and Tukana continuing on to his place in Lami. Salote had gone to work at the Tradewinds Hotel, where she was a bartender.

The detective immediately got on the phone to his office and asked for Vijay Dass, one of the people he had in mind to help with the Suva search for information on the Liga Ca and Seattle homicides.

Dass came on the line, and Tukana asked if he was involved in anything important.

"Not really, Dan. You got something going? I heard about your accident. It wouldn't have something to do with that, would it?"

"It might," replied Tukana. "I need to talk to you, meet somewhere, on the QT—okay?"

"Where do you want me, and when?"

"Now, come to my place."

"Okay, Dan. Half an hour."

"That's good, Vijay. Now tell me, is Sarita Chand there now?"

"Yeah, I saw her a few minutes ago."

"Why don't you see if she can come with you? Make some excuse for the two of you to get out of the office for a while."

When the two detectives arrived, Tukana asked if they would be interested in working on a confidential investigation. Dass said that it sounded interesting to him, and Chand said she would like to hear more. Tukana gave a rundown on the investigation. When he finished explaining the situation, they both agreed to sign on.

"Okay," said Tukana. "That's set then. Kabuta will arrange for you two to be assigned under me on a government project. I want you to do what you both do so well. Get into your usual haunts and start nosing around. Dig up the stoolies and lowlifes in Suva and see if you can raise some heat that might give us a lead on this Liga Ca gang. If we can find members of the group, maybe then we can find out the identities of the two men killed in Seattle. Who knows? Maybe their own people killed them. The only information we have on them is that they came from the Savusavu region a couple of years ago and that one of them is probably called Satala."

EIGHTEEN

Detective Sarita Chand walked along the waterfront on Stinson Parade, around Ratu Sukuna Park and past Tiko's Floating Restaurant that was built on what had once been a Blue Lagoon Cruise ship years before. The road passed over Nubukalou Creek and straight ahead across Usher Street to enter Suva Municipal Market.

The market covered a large area and was spread out on two floors, with a large number of stalls on the street level and many more above. All kinds of tropical fruits and vegetables were to be found in the market.

Sarita began to walk along the aisles between the vegetable and fruit stands, appearing to examine the goods but all the time watching the vendors and their customers. Eventually she made her way up to the second level and started to walk between the tables laden with yaqona.

Over in a dark corner of the building Sarita spotted a rather small Fijian man, unkempt, with graying and receding hair.

He noticed Sarita as she approached and turned to walk away down another aisle. She made a move to cross over and cut him off. He looked like he was going to make a run for it, but she raised a hand with the palm extended towards him, and he stood there as she approached.

"Tawake, I've got enough on you to put you away five times over, but right now I just want to talk to you. Come over here where we can have a quiet chat."

The Fijian followed her to a corner between the stalls. "I need to ask you some questions, and if you come up with useful answers and give me information I can use, then I might forget that I saw you today. If I think you're stalling then I'll run you in for theft, pick pocketing from tourists, pimping underage girls, selling marijuana and anything else I can think of."

"But I haven't been doing all those things. You know I haven't."

"Right now I only care about getting the information I need. I want to know about the Liga Ca."

Tawake reacted with a startled look.

"I know nothing about them. They're a secret gang, and nobody is allowed to even mention that name."

"Okay, Tawake, let's go for a ride. You're of no use to me any more, so you might just as well be taken off the streets for a while. I'm going to see it's for a long while."

"All right, I may know something, but we can't talk here," he whined quietly, looking around furtively.

"I'll pick you up in my car on Jellicoe Road. Be about half way along the King's Wharf in about ten minutes." She paused. "Tawake, you'd better show up or I'll hang you out to dry!"

After picking up her car in the parking lot off Central Street, she drove slowly down Stinson Parade and past the market again to Usher Street. There she turned left and then followed the road around to the right on Jellicoe Road, which led along King's Wharf. She drove slowly and let a few cars pass as she looked out for Tawake.

He suddenly appeared from behind a container box left off to the side. She pulled the car to a halt, and he quickly got in as she accelerated down the street.

"You're going to get me killed," he said, glaring at her.

"Quite possibly, but it's going to happen sooner or later anyhow." She grinned. "Would you rather have it happen on the outside, or do you want to take your chances in prison? The Liga Ca. What do you know about it?"

Tawake sat with his head down. "They are the most evil of all the bad men in Fiji. They have no respect for anyone, not even their own family, wives, children. They make no friends. They are dedicated to evil itself, evil for the sake of evil. They worship evil but have no idol to share, no altar to kneel at. They have no feelings, so they can't worship."

"How do I find them?" she asked. "Give me some names."

"You're a crazy woman!" said Tawake, raising his voice hysterically. "I can't mention any names or I'll die and die horribly. Do you think you can threaten me worse than they can?"

Sarita Chand gambled. "I'm going to tell you something, Tawake. These people I'm after will be after you too if you don't give me a lead. I'm going to spread the word that you gave me information that's going to lead me to them."

"You bitch, you can't do that! I did no such thing!"

"When my people set the street telegraph to work, who is going to be believed? You're a fool if you think your denials will get you anywhere. You'll be dead."

"Okay, okay. What do you want?"

"Names," she answered. "I want some names of members of this Liga Ca gang, and don't try to give me wrong names or the guys with the right names will come looking for you."

"I've heard Bobby Ledua mentioned, and Mohammed Faruk." He paused, and she waited before probing him again.

"Who else?"

"I don't know, maybe a guy called Chen Yung, and I can't remember any more."

"Okay, now one more name. Have you ever heard of a bad boy from the Savusavu region by the name of Satala?" She was watching his eyes and thought she saw them dilate slightly before he answered.

"Never heard of him," he replied quietly.

"You're lying," she screamed at him, causing him to jump in the seat.

"No! No! I'm telling you the truth. I've never heard that name."

She started to write in the notebook again and recited slowly as she wrote, "The above names given to me as members of Liga Ca gang by informant called Tawake."

"You bitch, you bitch."

"Now. What about a guy called Satala?"

"He was one of them," Tawake said. "I heard that he went somewhere for the gang, somewhere overseas."

She breathed a silent sigh of relief. "Was there anybody with him on this trip?"

"I think there was one other guy who went."

"Do you know the name of the other guy?"

"I'm not sure. It might have been Rakai or something like that, but I don't remember if I heard it right."

"Do you remember anything else about this group?"

"I've told you everything I know about them. For God's sake, don't let it out that you got it from me, or I'm a dead man."

Detective Chand dropped her informant at a bus stop and left him there. Then she drove to Fiji Police headquarters.

NINETEEN

Detective Vijay Dass was dressed as a dockworker and carried a card identifying him as a member of the Seamen's Union of Fiji.

He walked along the waterfront past a couple of freighters tied up at the King's Wharf, keeping his eyes open for some of the wharfies who were known to him, the ones that hopefully he could trust.

Eventually he saw a man who looked familiar sitting with some others having tea in the shade of a container. Strolling over to the group, he took out a cigarette and leaned over to get a light from the one he knew.

Dass turned the corner and waited for his contact to arrive.

"What do you want, Dass? I don't want to be seen with you, so make it quick," he said.

"As usual, I need some information, Mani. Do you know anything about a Fijian called Satala? He's from the Savusavu region. He might have been around here a few months ago."

"I remember somebody by that name, but I haven't seen or heard of him for a while. What's he supposed to have done?"

"Got himself killed. Do you remember who else he might have been hanging around with?"

"There were several bad guys he was around, but he was pals with one guy, name of Rakai, I think."

"What do you know about a group called Liga Ca?" asked Dass, watching the sudden fear in Mani's eyes.

"Man, I know nothing about them. Never heard of them. Now I got to go."

He rushed off. Dass looked after him for a few moments and then walked towards one of the freighters. He was impressed by Mani's reaction to the mention of Liga Ca. He would have to be careful how he asked about them.

He went along to the Seamen's Union office on the wharf and recognized the man at the counter from past investigations. No one else was in the office.

"How are you today?" he asked as the counterman turned to him.

"I'm fine. What can I do for you?" he asked.

"I'm trying to find out where a couple of old friends might be. Their names are Satala and Rakai. I thought they might have been working around the wharf, or maybe even shipped out from here."

"No, I haven't heard of them. Maybe you could try the wharf employment office down at the other end. If they were working on the loading docks, they wouldn't have been calling in here. I'm strictly on seamen's hiring, and I've nothing to do with wharfies."

Dass thanked him and went out of the office, but turned and stood by the open window outside. He heard the phone being picked up and a number being punched in.

A few moments later the counterman said, "Is this the Surfside?" Then after another few seconds, "Let me talk to Jawad Saliheen." He waited for Saliheen to pick up. "There was a guy here asking about Satala and Rakai. I told him I'd never heard of them." He listened for a moment. "I don't know who he is. But he smelled like a cop to me."

Detective Dass returned to police headquarters. Tukana had arrived just a few minutes earlier. After hearing the detective-sergeant's report, Tukana told Dass it was time to have a meeting of the group. He called Peter on his cell-phone and made the arrangement for him to be there with Ann. He contacted Sarita Chand. An hour later the five-some gathered at his place in Lami.

Tukana opened the meeting by giving a report of his time on the police computer, searching for terrorist activities in the Fiji Islands. The only thing found under terrorist activity was related to local gangs. "We've had quite a bit of information from our detective sergeants, and I'd like them to tell us of their findings. Sarita?"

"I spent the morning in the public market, where I hoped to find some of the informants I've used before," Sarita reported. "It took a while, but I spotted one by the name of Tawake. He gave up some members of the Liga Ca. I asked him if he'd heard of Satala, and at first he denied it. Then he said that Satala was a member of Liga Ca and he thought that they had sent him on some job overseas. I then asked if he knew of another guy who had made the trip with Satala, and he came up with somebody by the name of Rakai."

Tukana nodded to Detective Dass.

"I first found an old snitch of mine and managed to get a few words with him. He told me about Satala and his cobber, Rakai, which was about the same as Sarita had obtained from Tawake."

"Looks like Satala and Rakai were the two slashed throat victims in Seattle," Tukana said. "I'll try to find out more about them through the files." He directed himself to Sarita Chand. "You should follow-up on the names you got from your snitch. You and Dass should work this."

Tukana glanced at his notes. "Agent Eaton, this is where you come in. Can you get your FBI computers to work and see if you can come up with something on Jawad Saliheen? They'll do a worldwide search, but a good place to start might be Pakistan."

Ann nodded. "We can bring in the CIA and Secret Service as well. All the agencies are anxious to get results on this thing."

TWENTY

Detective Gerry McCann was getting more and more irritable as he lay in the hospital bed.

When Peter and Ann arrived to see him, they found him in a state of agitation worse than they had seen on previous visits. Peter was unable to settle him down and eventually left to consult with the neurosurgeon. They agreed it was probably better to take McCann out of the hospital and let him get back to work, as that might be the only way to simmer him down.

Peter went back and told Gerry they were going to take him back to Pacific Harbour. They made him promise to follow Peter's medical advice. On the way they brought him up to date about the work of the Fijian detectives.

When they arrived at Peter's villa, Ann Eaton hooked up to the main FBI computer system and put in a request for a search for "Jawad Saliheen." She also made a report to her boss in Seattle.

An hour or so later she went back through Fiji Internet to pick up mail and found encrypted messages for her from both the FBI search and also from George Paxton.

Paxton was impressed with the work of the Fijian detectives. He had started a search locally to find out more about Satala and Rakai. Now that he had their names, he could pursue an investigation of their time in Seattle and how they came into the country. If there was nothing to be found on them through the local immigration records, he would ask for help from the Canadians, as that would have been their next likely route to reach Seattle. Paxton asked Ann to have Tukana look into the records of Air Pacific and Air New Zealand.

Paxton added that he was also working on a search for Jawad Saliheen and Ahmed Aziz in case they had been in the Seattle area. At Ann's suggestion he had also begun a search on the other names that Detective Chand had shaken loose.

The report from the FBI computer revealed no information about the names she had submitted, but the search had been limited to domestic files. She got back to the FBI link and asked for the search to be extended to other countries, with emphasis on Pakistan, as suggested by Tukana.

Tukana, Dass and Chand were busy at the Suva police headquarters pursuing the names also.

Dass checked on the Surfside that turned out to be a rundown motel. It was some distance from the ocean with no surf in evidence. Dass and Tukana decided to go take a look. They signed out an unmarked car from the lot and drove around the seamier parts of Suva until they found the motel. Tukana saw a white Mazda parked by the side of the motel building. "I've seen that car a couple of times. Wonder where it was? We'll come back at dusk and check out the back. If we can find a place on the upper floor, we'll set up a stakeout."

Sarita Chand had been working on the Fiji Police computer while the others were out on their tour of the Surfside neighborhood. She had been looking through the files of the Fiji Police Department, the Prisons Service and the Judicial Department, submitting names of the Seattle victims and the Liga Ca members. With no positive results forthcoming, she had just about given up when she had an idea for another way to approach things. If she could not find anything about these people in the criminal files, then what about their identity prior to a criminal record? They would be going for anything they could get for free.

She went to the files on Social Welfare and began to search for the name "Satala." Again nothing.

She entered "Rakai" and up came the name "Rakai, Inosi" and also an address in the Savusavu area. Bingo! The application was about two years old.

She continued with the other names and found Bobby Ledua and Mohammed Faruk, two of the names her stoolie had mentioned.

TWENTY-ONE

McCann, Tukana and Dass, dressed in Telecom Fiji uniforms, were parked directly across the street from the Surfside Motel. The phone company truck had a cherry picker on it, which they had positioned near the top of a telephone pole. McCann and Dass were up in the bucket and had camera equipment with them in a toolbox. Dass had rigged a low shield with holes through which to shoot his pictures. With their backs to the motel, they were able to cover up their actions quite easily.

Tukana had remained at ground level inside the truck to watch the motel entrance. A large hat concealed his bandaged head, and he was also shielded by the newspaper that he was pretending to read. He could call to the men above when he saw anyone approaching.

Agent Eaton and Peter Barclay waited a few blocks away and Sarita Chand was nearby in Tukana's blue Ford in the other direction.

Ann Eaton's voice came through on the radio, calling to check in.

"We're in position on a side street about a half-kilometer or so beyond your location in Peter's gray Toyota. We're near a grocery store called Matt's."

When they had been there for about an hour, two men exited the motel. Dass got several pictures. They turned to walk along the street to where the white Mazda was parked. They got into the car, starting in the direction of Peter and Ann.

Tukana alerted them, "Two guys who look like Indians just came out of the motel. They got in a white Mazda and are coming your way. We'll be coming up behind them." He got out of the truck and walked along to join Chand in the Ford.

The white car proceeded along the street and passed the gray Toyota. Peter had started the engine and was ready to pull out and make a turn in pursuit when the Mazda pulled up to a small café just beyond the grocery store. The two men got out and entered.

Ann radioed, "They went into a café just past me."

"Okay," came back Tukana. "Follow them when they come out. These two may be the guys we want, so I'm going to move into position beyond you." Chand drove along to pass the café and park in a side street.

About a half hour later the two suspects came out of the café and strolled back to their car. They moved off, away from the motel. Ann and Peter followed.

They continued towards the city and, as the traffic increased, Peter had to move closer to the white car to avoid losing it. He remained one or two vehicles behind and, in his rear view mirror, could see Tukana's blue Ford had also moved up and was a few cars behind them.

The traffic began to thin out again as they moved into the suburbs. Eventually the road curved around on the side of a hill overlooking the city. The white Mazda slowed to a stop by a clearing with a view of Suva Harbour below.

Peter continued past the suspect's car, and Ann got on the radio to inform Tukana. Chand pulled in and parked by the side of the road around the corner short of the Mazda. Peter turned into a side street around the next corner, parking near the end of the street.

Ann got out and walked back to watch the white car through the hedge by the corner to see what the occupants were doing. The man on the passenger side was scanning the harbor area through binoculars, while the driver was looking over his partner's shoulder. She found a gap in the hedge to look down at the city and could see the ships moored along the waterfront. Coming across the bay and entering the harbor she could see a ship that was heading for the wharf area. It looked like a large ocean-going fishing trawler.

She went back to the car and called Tukana on the radio.

"They're parked, and one of them is using binoculars to scan the harbor," she told him. "It looks to me like they're interested in a big fishing boat that's just coming in across the bay and heading for the wharf."

"Okay," answered the Fijian detective. "You two keep on them when they move on. Chand and I are going to head down to the waterfront. If they come that way we'll be ready for them."

Ann was at the corner of the side street, watching through the hedge for the approach of the white car. When it appeared, she ran back and quickly jumped into the already moving Toyota. They came out of the side street to see the Mazda rounding the next corner and followed.

As expected, Peter and Ann found themselves going downhill in the general direction of Walu Bay and the waterfront.

"I expect they'll be headed for Prince's Wharf," said Peter. "That's where the large fishing boats tie up, from countries like China, Japan and Korea. It's around the corner from King's Wharf, where the large liners and freighters berth."

Ann got on the radio to Tukana to let them know the Mazda was heading in their direction.

"Okay," he answered. "We're waiting on Stinson Parade, where we can see the trawler when it comes in. There's space at the dock, so it's probably expected there. Keep us posted if they change direction."

Peter and Ann followed the car through Suva to the waterfront. It pulled in and parked by the side of the road near Tiko's Floating Restaurant at Sukuna Park. This was several hundred yards behind Tukana.

Peter went around the block to find a place where they could observe the Mazda from behind while separated by several cars. Ann called to let Tukana know their new location.

The trawler came into view around the corner where King's Wharf and Prince's Wharf met at right angles.

The prow of the hundred and ten foot vessel was dented and the hull was rusted and discolored. There were patches of red anti-rust undercoating paint along the sides and gray anti-foul along the waterline. The trawler looked tired and battered as she made her way slowly along to make a turn before finally nudging her bow into the space at the middle of the dock. The forward line was cast ashore and secured by a dockworker. The engine was reversed and, with the rudder hard over, the stern was drawn in to bring her alongside.

The red flag with yellow stars showed the ship's origin as Chinese. The name of the ship was faintly visible on the transom, "Sheng Yu 18."

The Chinese crew moved onto the dock to secure the lines, then went back aboard.

Tukana got on the radio. "Mac, you two can move on from there and take the truck back to Telecom Fiji. Tell Dass I need him here as soon as possible. Right now we're parked near Prince's Wharf, but we'll come to Fiji Telecom and pick him up when you get there with the truck."

After the ship had been tied up, the two men got out of the Mazda and walked along Stinson Parade, turning into

Usher Street to approach one of the gates of Prince's Wharf. They talked to the guard and after a few minutes were allowed in.

Tukana and Chand followed the men. Tukana presented his identification to the guard when they reached the gate. They passed through and headed along the wharf in the direction of the fishing trawler, but they stayed out of sight, moving from one cover to the next, using trucks and containers scattered around the dock.

The two men they were following continued to the side of the Chinese ship, but did not attempt to board it. They stood on the dock near the deckhouse, and eventually one of the crew approached. He turned away from them, and soon another man appeared that Tukana guessed was probably the captain. The three men talked for about ten minutes before the two men turned away and came back along the wharf.

Tukana and Chand retraced their path to the gate and hurried to their car, Tukana driving off before their quarry could spot them.

Tukana was on the radio to Ann even as they were pulling away.

"We had to move out," he told her. "The two guys went to the fishing boat, but are returning to their car now. Follow them if you can, and call us when you have them nailed down."

"Okay, will do."

Tukana and Chand continued around past King's Wharf to pick up McCann and Dass at Telecom Fiji.

Tukana leaned back towards Dass, talking over his shoulder as he drove. "Vijay, I want you to get in there and find out all you can about that Chinese trawler. We need to know where she's come from, how long she's supposed to be here and where she's going next. Maybe you can find one of your informants on the wharf and put him to work for you."

"I'll see what I can do, but she's just arrived and this may take a while."

"We may not have much time to spare," snapped Tukana. "If they've planned a fast turnaround, we might never find out what they're up to. They've to be dropping something off or picking something up would be my guess."

"Or some*one*," interjected McCann.

"That's a possibility too," agreed Tukana.

Dass knew the guards on the gate and spent some time talking with them before going through to the wharf. He learned from them that the trawler had come in for refueling and provisioning after having been at sea for the past six weeks. Her homeport was Wenling Township in the coastal province of Zhejiang. They said she was half loaded with fish at this stage of her voyage.

Dass moved along the wharf to the office, where a bunch of laborers hung around outside. He knew the usual boss at this site and was glad to find him inside when he entered.

"G'day Tom, how's it going?" he said to the man behind the desk.

"Not bad, Vijay. How's yourself?" he answered.

"Okay, thanks. Say, I need a little favor."

"You always do, Vijay," the employment manager said with a smile. "What is it this time?"

Dass closed the door.

"A Chinese trawler just came in, and I need to find out something about it. I want you to get me aboard when it's loading fuel or supplies."

"You're out of your mind, Vijay. That's more than my job's worth. They'd give me the axe for sure if I got caught sneaking you aboard."

"Tom, this is very important, and it's a matter of national security. I've orders to find out what's going on with that boat no matter what the cost."

"What do they suspect might be going on?" asked the manager.

"Don't know. But it's something big and very dangerous. That's all I can tell you except to add that my orders come from high up, and I can promise you no one will give you the axe for helping me. On the contrary, you might get in trouble if you don't help."

The manager was quiet for a few minutes as he sat thinking this over. He looked up at Dass standing across the desk.

"All right, Vijay. All I can do is add you to the provisioning gang when they go aboard."

"When is that supposed to happen?" asked Dass.

"This evening sometime. They've to give me the list of supplies they want, and then I've to get it filled first. I'd guess it'll be late tonight before we're ready to load things."

"Okay, Tom, thanks," said Dass, opening the door. "I'll be here this evening."

He turned back to the manager as he was stepping outside. "You're doing the right thing here. This is important."

Dass went back out the dock gate, crossed the street, and entered the bus station to call in to Tukana. "I've to be back this evening, and he's going to get me aboard with a provisioning gang. Maybe I can get a look around the boat and find out what's going on. The terrorists must be getting a delivery of something or sending something off that boat. The only way to find out what it is, or which way it's going, is to try to get a look around."

The group was at Tukana's place, examining the photos taken at the Surfside. The only ones that were recognized were Tawake, Chand's snitch, and the counter man at the Seamen's Union office that Dass had questioned. They thought that Bobby Ledua and Mohammad Faruk were probably among the unidentified men and that the only Oriental face was likely Chen Yung, the third gang member named by Tawake.

Ann suggested that the pictures be emailed right away to George Paxton with what little they had in the way of identification.

The discussion turned to the upcoming search of the Chinese fishing trawler and how they could help Dass in his task.

Tukana said, "We need a distraction to grab the crew's attention while Dass is on the boat, something that will give him the freedom to take a good look around. Anyone got an idea on how to create a diversion?"

TWENTY-TWO

The police cruiser was heading south when the police-woman driver noticed a green sedan coming out from a side street. The car did not stop at the corner as it made the turn on to the main thoroughfare. Officer Mary Tilbury turned on her flashing lights and increased her speed to come up behind the Dodge.

The green car pulled over to the side of the road, and Tilbury brought her cruiser to a stop behind it.

There were two men in the front and one in the back. The front occupants had dark skin and an Asian appearance; possibly East Indians or Pakistanis, she thought. A glance at the one in the back made her think that he was of Arab descent.

"May I see your driver's license and registration, please?"

"Certainly, officer, but what seems to be the trouble? Did I do something wrong?"

"Yes sir," she replied. "You failed to come to a stop at the corner when you made the turn back there. It's clearly marked with a stop sign."

The driver was fumbling in his wallet when Naida, from the back seat, shot Mary Tilbury in the head.

The driver pulled out quickly from the curb and raced down the road. Naida was breathing hard as the Buick rushed along.

"We must get there quickly," he said, finally. "But don't get stopped for speeding or making a stupid move like you just did back there. We can't afford to be caught or questioned at this stage." He paused as Hassan slowed the car.

"I want you to know I don't take kindly to having to work with morons like you, Hassan. And that applies to your colleague Harakh there as well. If we didn't need you here, I'd find a way to lose both of you. Your stupidity could have gotten us arrested back there and put an end to the great plan which we have to attack the Americans here."

The two men in the front, Rakif Hassan and Aktar Harakh, cringed. They had seen others eliminated because of Naida's wrath.

It took only a few minutes for a passerby to call in the shooting.

Two cruisers arrived, followed by two detectives in a third car. The scene was cold. But the recording of Officer Tilbury's call in gave them the color and make of the car and the license number.

A police bulletin was broadcast on TV and radio within thirty minutes, asking for information on a green Dodge that might have been seen in the region of Rainier and possibly heading south at the time of the killing. One of the many calls this generated was from a woman in Renton who told of a green Dodge at her neighbor's house.

Two detectives arrived at the woman's house within the hour and were not surprised to find an older female answering the door. They presented their badges and asked to come in.

One of the detectives did the questioning while the other listened and took notes.

"Are the men home at the moment, Mrs. Doyle?"

"I don't think so. I saw them leave in a taxi some hours ago and I haven't seen them return."

"How long have they lived next door?"

"I don't know exactly, but about three or four weeks I think."

"How many men are living there?"

"I see three regularly. Dark-skinned men, but they didn't look like blacks. Others have come to the house from time to time, but I don't think they lived there."

"Is the green Dodge the only car you've noticed there?"

"It's the one I usually see, but there have been different cars parked outside when they've had visitors."

"Do you happen to have noticed the name on the taxi that picked them up today?"

"Oh yes," she answered with a smile. "It was an Airport taxi from Seatac Cab Company. I noticed because my late husband used to use them when he was going out of town."

The detectives crossed the street. No one answered the doorbell. They looked through the window at the side of the detached garage, and inside they could see a green Dodge sedan. Through another small window at the back of the garage they were able to read the number on the front plate of the car, and this was duly entered in the notebook. The number was the one they were looking for.

When they returned to the squad room, they reported to the Chief of Detectives. He sent them for a warrant, and after listening to the description of the bad guys, told them to coordinate with Matt Benson of The Counter Terrorist Squad.

They found Benson in his office, going through a pile of paper work. He looked up as they knocked and entered.

They told Benson of their investigation in Renton.

"I sure hope you're onto something that could connect with the airport terrorist thing," he said, standing up as he pushed the papers in front of him into a stack. "Did you get your search warrant?"

"All approved. The Chief of Detectives wants you in on this."

"See you in ten minutes at your car."

When they got to the Renton place, they parked a hundred yards away and went to visit Mrs. Doyle again to ask if anyone had returned to her neighbor's house while they had been gone. She said she'd seen no one.

Benson showed her the picture of Sayed Naida that the Brits had sent.

"Yes," she said excitedly. "He's one of them—from across the street I mean."

The detectives split up to cover the front and back doors.

Benson tried the front door, and it was unlocked. They entered with guns drawn, but found no one. The three of them went through the empty house. The place was a mess, empty food containers, bottles and newspapers.

While the detectives tagged and bagged, Benson went out to the garage. He went through the car, but could only come up with a parking receipt stuck behind a sun visor.

When they went back to the squad room, they started checking on the real estate. The house was rented from an agency in Renton on behalf of the owner, who was living in Arizona. The owner had not had any direct contact with the renter, who had called the agency in answer to an ad in the *Seattle Times*.

They also ran the records of the Seatac Cab Company, which did have a record of the fare from the house. The driver said he had delivered three men from there to downtown Seattle, dropping them off at the Four Seasons Hotel. He prided himself on guessing people's countries of origin because of his years working the airport.

"Two of them looked Indian, but the other one was an Arab," he said confidently.

The Four Seasons showed no evidence of registration by the three men.

Benson sat at his desk and looked at the parking ticket he had found in the Dodge. It turned out to be from the Seatac short time parking lot for the same day on which the FBI had had the fiasco with the terrorists at the airport.

The detective reached for the phone and called George Paxton.

"We've had an officer killed on a traffic stop for a simple moving violation thing," began Benson. "Well, we were lucky and got a lead to a house in Renton, where we found the car. The license number was the same one reported by the officer. I went over the vehicle and found something of interest to you. It's a parking receipt that was behind the passenger side sun visor. George, the ticket is from the Seatac short time parking and is dated the same day that you had the shooting out there."

"Where's the car now?" asked Paxton.

"They're bringing it in to the police garage to give it a complete going over. They'll be doing the house too."

"I want to know everything they find," said Paxton. "Do you have anything on the occupants?"

"That's the other interesting thing, George. According to the taxi driver who picked them up, two of the three men who were stopped by our officer looked like East Indians and the third looked like an Arab. I showed the picture of Naida that you got from London to the neighbor, and she recognized him as one of the three, the one who looked like an Arab."

"Goddamn, Ben, this is the first lead we've had on these guys since the shooting. Let's hope you find something else in the house or the car that'll help."

The green Dodge was brought to the police garage, where it was gone over for fingerprints inside and out. The visors, glove compartment inside lining, inner surfaces of the trunk lid and hood where they might be grasped for opening, gas cap, rear view mirror back, and other sites which might have been missed were all dusted. The experts went over the house looking for a match with the prints found in the car.

Ultimately they decided that three individuals had been occupants of the house and the car, other fingerprints being found in only one or the other but not both.

The car was then searched completely and in the process disassembled. Not much of interest was discovered in the search except for a sliver of paper that looked like the flap of an envelope. This was found when the dashboard was removed, and it appeared to have fallen through one of the slits of a heater vent. There was some writing on it. It read "15/8 AP FJ."

TWENTY-THREE

Detective Vijay Dass passed through the gate to the Prince's Wharf at about ten p.m. and went into the wharf office to see the manager.

"Everything on schedule, Tom?"

"As far as I know, Vijay. But I hope there isn't going to be any trouble."

"Me too, my friend. However, there'll be a small distraction to hold the crew's attention."

"You're crazy, Vijay. You're going to get yourself killed."

"Not if things go right. When does the food service lorry get here?"

"Should be before eleven. They wouldn't have come that late, but the Chinese insisted they get it done tonight so they can leave at dawn."

"Wonder what their rush is?" asked Dass.

"I'd guess they don't want to pay for anymore tie-up time than they have to. They've already taken on fuel this evening and, since no repairs are necessary, they just want to get out of here."

"Seems unusual," Dass said. "You'd think they'd want to take a few days off before heading out again."

"Who knows?"

At about fifteen minutes before eleven p.m., the supply van came through the gate and pulled up at the wharf office. There were two men aboard, the driver and his helper. Both came into the office.

The wharf manager explained that Dass was the agent for the Chinese and that he would be with them as they loaded the supplies on the fishing boat. He dealt with the driver's paperwork, and he and Dass signed the receipts.

The two supply men and Dass then went out to get in the van and drive along the wharf towards the fishing trawler.

As they moved away from the office, a blue Ford entered through the wharf gate. Tukana presented his credentials to the guards. Chand and McCann were also in the car, and all three got out when they reached the manager's office.

As they entered, the manager looked up and groaned.

"As if Dass wasn't enough, you have to show up, Tukana."

"Now, now, Tom. Don't get all riled up," said Tukana with a smile. "We just have a little job to do."

"I hope I don't have to be part of it, that's all," said the wharf boss.

"We're going to leave you out of it."

The manager was groaning again as they left the office.

The supply van pulled up by the side of the trawler, and Dass got out with the driver and his helper. They went around to the back of the vehicle, and the driver opened the door. Two crewmen standing by the rail watched them, but made no move to come ashore as the three men began to unload the supplies, placing the boxes and sacks on the dock behind the van.

Dass picked up a barrel near the back door. Assisted by the driver, he hoisted it on his shoulder. He turned towards the ship's side, and the two crewmen watched him suspiciously but did not try to stop him as he crossed the short plank to climb aboard. He stopped as he approached them and turned his free hand palm upward in a questioning gesture, asking where the supplies were to be stowed. One of the deckhands pointed aft, and Dass turned to head in that direction. The two Chinese, who made no effort to help him, followed along behind.

He found an open hatch as he rounded the corner of the deckhouse and, assuming this to be his objective, turned to climb down the ladder inside. At the bottom was another crewman, who waited till he had reached the lower deck, then pointed to a large locker on the other side. Dass entered and lowered his barrel to set it on the deck against the others sitting there.

The detective scanned the locker and its contents and also stopped to survey the lower deck area before mounting the ladder to go back up to the main deck. The crewman watched him closely as he was looking around. The area was poorly lit and he could not see much, but it appeared to lead aft to what was probably the crew's quarters.

The other two were starting to carry the supplies aboard and Dass formed a chain with them, the driver carrying from the van to the side of the ship, the helper from the plank aft to the hatch opening and Dass down the ladder to stow the supplies in the locker as directed by the crewman.

Dass noticed there was some activity on the other side of the vessel and forward of the deckhouse. He could not make out what was going on, but two men were leaning over the side, and he could hear the sound of sloshing water. He was unable to investigate, as the men on deck were coming towards him. He pulled out his cigarettes and, after placing one between his lips, gestured with the package towards the crewmen. They each took a cigarette without smiling and he struck a match to light all three.

Suddenly there was a shout from the driver, who was at the back of the van. They saw flames and smoke coming from a shed across the dock. There were shouts in Chinese from the two crewmen standing with Dass. This brought the others to the shore side of the vessel, including the man from below and those who had been leaning over the other rail.

Dass moved forward and rounded the front of the deckhouse to cross over to the seaward rail. He could see a boat lying alongside in the darkness. There were two men aboard holding on to lines hanging from the side of the fishing trawler. He pulled his head back to avoid being seen and went forward again, crossing to the side of the hold that was open on the port side. He looked in and saw large containers that he assumed were refrigerated for packing fish.

One of the containers lay open, and inside was a large oblong box.

Dass looked over to the other side of the ship. The crewmen were still watching the fire. He could hear the wailing of sirens in the distance.

He eased himself over the side of the hold and let himself drop on to the deck below. He moved over to the open container and inspected the box. There was nothing written on it and no label to indicate its contents.

Dass was turning away from the box when he was struck on the head with a crowbar. He died instantly.

The distraction created by the fire and the firefighter action, meant to cover Dass's movements, now became the ally of the Chinese. The crewmen from the main deck returned to the port side and, under cloud cover that provided a starless and moonless night, the box was hoisted out of the hold and lowered over the side into the waiting boat.

The two men with the supply van finished loading the supplies on board the trawler. Returning to the van, they closed the rear door. They drove out past the smoldering shed that had been well doused by the firemen and stopped at the manager's office to complete their paperwork. Tukana, Chand and McCann were waiting there.

"Where's the agent who went with you?" asked Tukana when the driver walked in.

"I've no idea," the driver said. "He helped us load most of the stuff and then disappeared. We thought maybe he'd gone to see the captain, but we couldn't find him, so we left."

"Where was he when you saw him last?"

"Having a smoke with a couple of the Chinese crewmen. Then the fire broke out, and we were watching that for a while. Never saw him after that."

Tukana took out his cell phone and put through a call to Kabuta. The CID Director answered sleepily with a disgruntled "Yes." Tukana grimaced.

"Sorry to disturb you, sir. This is Tukana, and I've a situation that you should know about."

"Yes, Tukana, what is it?"

Tukana told him about the attempt to search the fishing trawler and of Dass's failure to return.

"What do you propose to do now?" asked Kabuta. "You're going to have to be careful how you go about searching for him on board the trawler. That would be considered as foreign territory to Fiji authorities as far as the Chinese Embassy people are concerned. They would say it's not in your jurisdiction."

"Yes sir. I thought that would be the case. I was going to ask to see the captain and then request his permission to look around because we have a report of a missing man who was last seen aboard."

"Okay, Tukana. But you're going to have to use a lot of tact in your approach, and make sure you don't say anything out of place. All we need is a diplomatic incident rearing its ugly head. I don't want to be getting calls from the P.M. because he's heard from the Chinese Embassy."

Tukana rounded up a couple of wharf security men, and they went aboard the trawler. The captain was reluctant to cooperate, but eventually complied when he was told that a man who was bringing supplies on his ship had disappeared.

Tukana and his men started at the back rail and worked their way forward to the deckhouse. Two crewmen were with them, and the captain had them move various items on the deck that might possibly have concealed a man.

They went down the ladder to the storage lockers, and these were opened and searched. Going aft on the lower deck, they entered the crew's quarters, where men were disrupted from their sleep when the lights were turned on. They were made to stand aside as Tukana, accompanied by the captain, searched the area.

Tukana went forward to the hold, and the crewmen opened one side of the hatch cover. There was a ladder inside, and one of the crewmen led the way down to the floor of the hold, turning on the lights below. The captain followed. There was no sign of Dass. They opened refrigerated containers that appeared to be full of ice and frozen fish. Other containers, that were not refrigerated, were empty.

The detective finally had to give up the search and went ashore.

Tukana pulled out his cell phone and called Kabuta to give him a report on the search of the ship.

"Well, you did what you could, and we can only guess that they've disposed of Dass somewhere. We've no idea if he's still on that ship or if they got him off during the hubbub with the fire. There's not much more we can do about it at this time."

"Can't we do something to hold the ship?" asked Tukana. "They plan to leave at dawn."

"No, we've got nothing to hold them, on and we can't start a political mess with the Chinese. Their embassy would really have a field day with us. The search was bad enough without trying to hold their ship under arrest. No, we'll just have to let them go, much as I regret it." Kabuta sounded frustrated.

"It's a terrible thing to lose a man like this, and we don't even know what's happened to him," Tukana said.

"We'll meet at your place at about eight o'clock. Get the whole team there and we'll discuss this. Goodnight, Tukana." Kabuta hung up.

TWENTY-FOUR

When McCann returned to Pacific Harbour, Peter and Ann Eaton were having dinner by the pool. There were candles on the table.

"We didn't know when you'd be back," Peter said.

"Sorry for interrupting," McCann smiled.

"What's doing on the case?" Ann asked.

"Things didn't go so well," said McCann. "Dass went aboard the trawler and disappeared. We couldn't find him anywhere." He sat down wearily.

"That's bad news," she said. "What do you suppose happened to him?"

"I'm afraid the Chinese caught him searching their boat and took care of him. We have no idea what they did to dispose of him, but it looks bad. Kabuta is afraid to hold the ship without just cause, since it would create a big stink with the Chinese Embassy and blow our whole investigation."

Peter went in to get McCann a beer, which he accepted gratefully, saying, "Vinaka, mate."

Ann watched him chug the beer. "There's been quite a bit of police action in Seattle. A woman officer, Mary Tilbury, stopped a car for a moving violation, and one of the occupants shot her dead at the scene. Later, Seattle PD got a lead that took them to a house in Renton, where they found the car, but the suspects were long gone. Turns out that two of the suspects might have been Indian or Pakistani and the third looked like an Arab."

"And they've no idea where to find these guys now?" McCann asked.

"There were a couple of other things that came out in the search of the car. They found a stub from the Seatac parking garage that would have put the car there on the day that the FBI had the action when Kerrigan and one of the terrorists got killed." She stopped to look at him.

"And what was the other thing?" asked McCann.

"They found a bit of paper with some writing on it that may or may not mean anything," she replied. "It said '15/8 AP FJ.'"

"What do they suppose that means?" asked the detective.

"They didn't offer any suggestions. But I guess they think that the 'FJ' might stand for 'Fiji' and hope we might figure out the rest of it, if it does in fact relate to Fiji."

"Well, we'll have to give it some thought, but right now we'd better hit the sack," said McCann. "We've to be at Tukana's place at eight for a meeting with Kabuta, and that's only a few hours away."

They arrived at Tukana's place a little after eight and found Detective Sarita Chand already there. Kabuta arrived shortly afterwards.

The talk centered around all that had happened since their last meeting. Dass's disappearance was debated, and no one could explain how he had suddenly vanished without a trace.

"We don't know if they got him off the ship somehow or if they still have him aboard," Kabuta said. "Anyhow, probably we'll never know now because they're gone. They pulled out this morning at dawn, and there's nothing we could do to stop them."

He looked at the glum faces around the table.

"We shall all miss Dass," finished Kabuta. "He did his job well."

The Director then went on, "Is there any further information on the local terrorist situation?" He was looking at Tukana now.

"We emailed the pictures taken at the Surfside Motel to the FBI through Ms. Eaton, but they haven't had time to respond on that yet, have they, Ann?" enquired Tukana.

"No, sir. They forwarded the photos to all the agencies, but we've had no response yet."

"Is there anything else from them?"

Ann told them about the Seattle P.D. action and the findings she had already related to Peter and McCann at the villa. She finished by telling of the scribbled note that was found containing the numbers and letters "15/8 AP FJ."

"'15/8' might be a date," said Kabuta. "In this part of the world, we put the day before the month, so it probably indicates the fifteenth of August. That's only two days from now."

"And we probably all agree that FJ stands for Fiji," suggested Tukana.

"The letters AP are most likely to indicate 'Air Pacific,'" offered Sarita Chand.

"Okay," said Kabuta. "So far we have the idea that these probably Islamic guys in Seattle may be interested in something happening, possibly in Fiji, conceivably involving Air Pacific and maybe on August fifteenth. Is that it?"

They all looked at him, waiting.

"I've no argument with your scenario," he said after a pause. "But we mustn't accept it as fact and put too much weight on it. We have to discuss it and look for other possible meanings."

"I've a thought that's been bothering me," said McCann.

"What's that, Mac?"

"Well, it seems to me that since the trawler came in here and stayed for just one night, they had to be dropping something off or picking something up. Now that's a sizable ship, so whatever it transported is probably sizable too. If the item were small, then it could have been brought in or taken out in luggage and probably on an airline. There's got to be a reason why it wasn't handled by a regular airline flight or by airfreight, and the only reason I can think of is because it's too damn big."

"So what are you suggesting?" Kabuta said.

"I'm suggesting that we ought to be looking for a ship with a name indicated by the letters 'AP,'" answered McCann.

Tukana got up and went to a pile of newspapers on the other side of the room. He came back to the table with one of the papers. "The *Fiji Times* has all the local shipping news each Wednesday. Maybe there's an answer here."

They went on discussing the note, trying to find other interpretations, while Tukana scanned the paper. After several minutes he suddenly said, "Listen!" and they were silent as he looked around the table.

"There's a container ship due in Suva tomorrow. She's scheduled to depart on August fifteenth for North America and her final outgoing port of call is Seattle, Washington." He paused before looking around the group again.

"Her name is the *Austral Pioneer*," he announced.

"What shipping line?" asked Kabuta.

Tukana checked. "Pacific Container," he said and then added, "They're represented here by Fiji Shipping, Limited."

"That's good," said Kabuta. "I happen to be a good friend of the Managing Director of Fiji Shipping, Paul Temple. Maybe we can get some help from him in finding out about the *Austral Pioneer* and what she's loading here for America."

"We don't have much time," put in Tukana. "She's leaving only two days from now."

"Since that limits the chances of finding what they're shipping before they load it," Peter said, thinking out loud, "maybe we'd better plan on having someone aboard when she leaves."

"Yes," agreed Kabuta. "You're right, of course, and we have to plan that now. Getting somebody aboard can't be done at the last moment as she's pulling out."

He looked around the table. "Do any of you have any suggestions for a cover?"

McCann spoke up again. "Some of these freighters carry a small number of passengers. Does the *Austral Pioneer* happen to be one of those?"

"As a matter of fact, she does have accommodation for ten or twelve passengers," said Sarita Chand.

McCann had been looking pensive and now spoke up again. "This has to be a good cover. We can't have a cop suddenly appear on board as a last minute passenger. I was thinking…"

"Yes, Mac, what is it?" Kabuta prompted.

"Well, how about a doctor and his wife who are winding up their vacation and decide to take a leisurely voyage home on a freighter?"

Peter and Ann stared at McCann like he had suddenly gone out of his mind.

Peter's mouth dropped open. "Are you suggesting that Ann and I go on the ship as husband and wife for the trip to Seattle?"

"We're down to the last resort, old buddy. You tell me a better way to get someone aboard to snoop around and find out what's being sent to Seattle to create havoc there. We're out of options, and we're sure as hell out of time at this end."

Peter turned to look at Ann. "I'll do whatever's necessary," she said, and Peter nodded.

"Okay, then it's settled," said Kabuta. "The doctor and Agent Eaton will go aboard the ship as husband and wife and try to find out what's being sent to Seattle from here. But we haven't ruled out the possibility that the 'AP' could stand for Air Pacific. Do they've a flight to the U.S. on the fifteenth?"

"Yes, they do," Sarita said. "It leaves in the evening and gets into Los Angeles in the morning. That's on the same date because of the dateline change."

"Okay then," continued Kabuta. "We should have somebody on that flight to keep an eye out for one or more of our friends from the Surfside."

"I guess that would be me," volunteered McCann. "I'd be the logical one." He paused and then added, "Besides, my vacation time is about over."

Kabuta smiled. "We'll miss you, Mac, but you seem to be the best one for this job."

Tukana looked around the group and then said to Kabuta, "This is breaking up my team, sir."

"I know you're making a joke, Dan, but unfortunately that already happened when they got Dass." There was silence in the group for several moments before Kabuta continued.

"You'll have to visit your friend, the Chargé, again, Miss Eaton. He'll need to get you and the doctor some new passports indicating your marital status under an alias. This must be done right away, and I hope that he can accommodate you without delay."

Kabuta ordered Tukana and Chand to set up a watch on the Surfside to keep an eye on the men who had visited the Chinese trawler. He wanted to know where they were going next, possibly on the freighter or on the Air Pacific flight to Los Angeles.

TWENTY-FIVE

Kabuta made a call to his friend, Paul Temple, at Fiji Shipping. He was already at work and said he would be available to meet with the CID Director if he wanted to come by. Kabuta wanted to talk to him in person.

Fifteen minutes later they were together in Temple's office, and a young woman appeared with a tray of coffee and rolls.

"What's up, Isi?" asked the shipping company director, using the nickname rarely heard in the presence of CID personnel. "What do you need from me?"

"I'm sure that you have guessed it's important," Kabuta said.

Temple nodded with a smile, and waited for his friend to continue.

Kabuta gave him a fairly detailed recital of the events to date, stressing how extreme the threat was if the terrorists managed to get a weapon of mass destruction into position in a major metropolitan area in America.

He explained that there was a possibility of such a device being loaded on the *Austral Pioneer* in Suva for delivery to the target area.

"We think they're going to hit Seattle, and the docks there are pretty well centrally located in the city," he ended.

There was silence as Temple digested the enormity of the situation. When he spoke, his voice quavered.

"We'll have to search the whole ship right away," he managed.

"No good. You must understand, Paul, that if these people find out we're on to them, they'll do anything to make their statement whenever and wherever they can. If they have the capability for mass destruction in their hands, they'll use it here rather than lose it. They might not kill as many people here as in Seattle, but the result would still be horrendous."

"What do you want me to do?" asked Temple resignedly.

"We want you to put two of our people aboard as passengers. We think they might be able to find out what's been put aboard and deal with it one way or the other while the ship is out at sea."

"Who are the lucky two?" asked Temple.

"Doctor Peter Barclay, whom you know, and an FBI agent who will travel as his wife."

"Holy Christ!" exploded the shipping chief. "Of course, I know Peter! But why is he involved in this thing?"

"It's a long story. They'll travel incognito, of course, and we figured the 'doctor and his wife returning from vacation' was a good cover story. We know the terrorists will have some of their people aboard, and their identities have to be revealed before the ship gets to Seattle. We need to find both the device and the people who are going to activate it."

"Okay, Isi," Temple said, reaching for a pad on his desk. "I'll get them a passage on the ship. The passenger cabins are not all occupied, fortunately."

He started writing and then stopped to look at Kabuta.

"What names are they going under?" he asked.

"It'll be Doctor Simon Armour and his wife, Elizabeth. They've gone to see the American Chargé d'Affairs to get passports in those names. We hope he can do it right away."

"I'll have to present them as personal friends to get them aboard at this late date," said Temple as he wrote down the names. "Otherwise it's going to look fishy."

Peter and Ann went to the American Embassy, dropping McCann in the city en route as he wanted to do some shopping. They got in to see the Chargé right away, having called first from Tukana's place.

Craig Kendall listened to their story in his office with the door closed and looked nervous as he listened to Ann Eaton tell of the goings on of the previous few days, including the tailing of the terrorist suspects and the arrival of the Chinese trawler. When he heard about the disappearance of Dass and the possibility of a weapon of mass destruction being transferred to the container ship, he looked flustered.

"What are you going to do about this?" he asked Ann.

"We're hoping to go aboard the *Austral Pioneer* under cover in an attempt to find out who the terrorist agent or agents are on board and what device they're concealing. The goal is to deal with the situation before the ship reaches Seattle and, if possible, while she's still at sea."

"I see. What can I do to help?" he asked.

"We need you to set us up with fake passports," Ann said. "And we need them today," she added before he got a chance to respond.

He reached for the intercom to ask his secretary to bring in application forms. "Is there anything else you need from me?"

"Yes sir. We need a couple of hand guns and a Geiger counter."

Kendall sighed. "The Marine contingent should have those. Anything else?"

"Yes sir," answered Ann. "I need to call my chief in Seattle again on your secure line."

They left Kendall's office, Ann to make her call to Seattle and Peter to start filling in the passport applications.

She got through to Paxton right away, and he was glad to hear from her. She brought him up to date on the action in Fiji, and he listened as she told of Dass's disappearance and the suspicious actions suggesting that the Chinese trawler might have been delivering a terrorist weapon.

"We think there's a chance they might be putting the device on a container ship heading for Seattle," she continued. "And undoubtedly they have agents aboard if that's the case. The ship is called the *Austral Pioneer*,which fits with the 'AP' on the note."

"So how do you propose we handle this?" asked Paxton.

"Peter Barclay and I are going to make the trip to Seattle aboard the freighter as Doctor Simon Armour and wife, Elizabeth. Of our group we seemed to be best suited, and all agreed it was a reasonable cover."

"It sounds very risky," said Paxton. "I wish you were with one of our other agents."

"There's no time for that, sir. Besides, since he really is a doctor, that helps to make the cover story more secure."

"I've some information for you and your Fijian friends," said Paxton, changing the subject. "We got a make on the two whose pictures you emailed. It turns out that they're from Pakistan, one called Jawad Saliheen and the other Ahmed Aziz. Both are members of the Islamic World Federation. I'll send their labeled pictures through on email to your friend in the Fiji Police Department if you give me his address."

"That's terrific," she said. "Tukana will be very pleased." She gave him Tukana's email address.

"We also got pictures of other members of the Islamic World Federation bunch, and we're going to run these by the witnesses, a neighbor and a cab driver, who identified Naida from his picture. Maybe they'll recognize a couple of them as the companions who lived with him. They were there when he killed the traffic cop the other day."

"That's good news," she said. "Hope it works out."

"Okay, Ann," concluded Paxton. "Take care of yourself, and you'd better call me tomorrow before you go aboard in case something else comes up in the meantime."

"One other thing," she added. "McCann is taking the Air Pacific flight tomorrow night for L.A. There's always a chance that the 'AP' on the scrap of paper meant Air Pacific instead of *Austral Pioneer* and maybe some of the terrorists are flying instead of sailing."

"I'll look forward to seeing him and getting a full report when he gets back. Call me tomorrow."

Peter and Ann finished the applications and left the Embassy with a bag containing pistols and ammunition and also a hand-held Geiger counter. They drove to Cardo's, where they were to meet McCann for lunch.

They chatted over the meal and talked about meeting up in Seattle. However, with the continuing threat facing them, there was an undercurrent of feeling suggesting that the imminent farewell might be a final one.

TWENTY-SIX

Paul Temple drove them to the *Austral Pioneer* since they were supposed to be friends of his. He told them that the containers loaded in Fiji were in the upper tier and aft in the stack on the port side. He escorted them aboard and introduced them to Captain Desmond Watt, a gracious Englishman.

The captain of the *Austral Pioneer* gave a slight bow as he shook hands.

"Welcome aboard Doctor, Mrs. Armour. I hope we can make you comfortable and that you enjoy a pleasant voyage with us."

They were shown to their stateroom, which they found to be quite spacious. Ann saw Peter looking at the twin beds and smiled. She put her hand on Peter's.

"Hang tough, husband of mine."

"I'll do my best."

"I'm sure you will, Peter. I'm sure you will."

They went out on the small deck area aft at the "D" deck level on the port side when the ship was leaving and watched the tugs working. Watching as the waterfront receded, their thoughts were unspoken, but both were wondering when they would see Fiji again.

They met all their fellow passengers at the cocktail hour in the lounge and enjoyed dinner with the Captain, the Chief Engineer and a couple from South Australia. Dinner conversation was pleasant, as was the wine. Following the meal everyone moved back to the lounge for after dinner drinks, some playing cards and others watching a video.

Peter and Ann returned to their cabin around eleven.

"Better set the alarm," said Ann. "We have to look for the containers that came aboard in Suva, and early morning seems like a good time to nose about—before too many people are around."

They were up shortly before dawn and, going down to the main deck level, they exited on the port side, finding themselves looking up at the stack of containers, three tiers high.

"Okay," said Peter. "Tukana said they would be marked with a blue sticker at the lower right corner on each side."

They walked forward on the port side of the stack and found the boxes with a blue sticker at the lower right corner. Four were placed in the upper tier and beneath, in the second tier, were the other six. It was apparent that the ship was not fully loaded. There were gaps between some of the containers, especially in the upper tier.

"Well, we found them all," said Peter. "Now what?"

"If there's a device aboard, they could be planning to unload it in LA and then move it by road to Seattle."

One of the crew approached. Ann put her hand on Peter's shoulder. When the seaman had passed she turned as if nothing had occurred.

"I must make a call to my boss," she said.

"I guess we have to go to the bridge," answered Peter. "That's where the ship's communication center is located."

"I won't have a secure line this time," she said. "But I can handle that."

They went up to the bridge and entered the command center of the *Austral Pioneer*.

At this hour, during the forenoon watch, the Third Officer was on duty.

"Good morning sir, madam," he said as they came in. "Welcome to the bridge. I'm Third Officer Richard Martin."

"I'm Doctor Simon Armour, and this is my wife, Elizabeth," said Peter. "It looks so complicated. Can you explain some of it?"

The officer showed them the navigational and steering equipment on the bridge and answered the many questions that they both had as he went from one item to another.

Aft of the navigational part of the bridge was a small room containing the ship's communications gear. This included Telex as well as the ship's computer and radiotelephone equipment. Faxes, phone calls and Internet messages were sent on a Comsat-B system, and these were transmitted through a geostationary satellite 30,000 kilometers above the earth.

"Can I make a phone call to the U.S?" asked Ann.

"Certainly, ma'am. It'll cost you about four dollars a minute," he answered.

He showed her the phone and set it up for her to use.

"Just dial the number and you should get through," he said. "I'll be out here if you need me." With that he left to return to the chart table on the bridge.

Ann put in the numbers of Paxton's direct line and soon heard it ringing.

He answered with an abrupt "Yes?"

"Hello, Dad. It's Liz," she said in a loud voice.

"Yes. Hello, dear. How are you?" he responded cheerfully.

"We're fine. Simon and I are enjoying our cruise so far. The accommodations are very good and the food so far has been fine.

"There are eight other passengers from different home-lands, which makes it interesting. Let's see now. We have Professor Jonathon and Mrs. Maria Calvert. He's in Economics at Stanford. Henri and Claudette Marquand are from Morocco, where he teaches at a university in Rabat. Larry Johnson and his wife Ellie from Adelaide are in the wine business, which is nice for Simon who is into wines. Then we also have two individual passengers who are round trippers. One is a widow lady, Mrs. Mary Kirkpatrick, who hails from Galveston and is on her third freighter trip. The other is Dr. Carroll Munson from Israel. He's a Ph.D. in Humanities at Tel Aviv University, where he's in the Department of Arabic Language and Literature and specializes in Islamic Traditions."

Agent Eaton went on as if she was answering enthusiastic questions. "I wouldn't say exciting, but it's been very interesting to see how things work on a container ship. They loaded ten containers in Suva. Two are reefers—see how I know the technical terms?" she laughed.

"Good for you. How do I get a hold of you?"

"You can call the ship on the phone or send a fax by satellite. There's also a computer system, so you can send an email if you wish. I've a card here with the numbers and the address."

She read off the information to Paxton, and after some more chat with "Dad," they said good-bye and ended the call.

TWENTY-SEVEN

Paxton set down the phone and called his secretary on the intercom.

"Pam, get the Director's office on the phone, and tell them I need to talk with him as soon as possible."

"Yes, sir, right away," she answered, starting to make the call as he finished speaking.

Within a few minutes she called him back. "The Director is on the line right now."

Paxton grabbed for the phone. "Yes, Mr. Director. Further to my report on the action in Fiji?"

"Yes, Paxton. What's going on there?"

"We suspect that the Islamic terrorists who were being followed there by the Fijian authorities and some of our people may have had a nuclear device brought in on a fishing boat."

"Yes, yes, Paxton. I received that in your report."

Paxton was relieved to know that his report had reached the Director himself.

"We suspect they may have loaded the weapon on a container ship, the *Austral Pioneer*, which left Suva last evening, local time, and is heading for Seattle by way of L.A. I've just heard from our agent on the container ship that ten containers were loaded in Suva and they have them tagged, but haven't as yet been able to search them."

There was a pause before the Director continued.

"Did the agent have anything else to report?"

"She gave us a list of the other passengers, and some of them sound interesting. There's a couple from Morocco and also a doctor from Tel Aviv, who has as a main interest the study of Islamic traditions."

"Okay, Paxton. I want you here in D.C. right away. This whole thing has to be discussed at a meeting of the Special Counter Terrorism Commission. Get here as soon as you can. If there's no direct flight within a couple of hours, then have the Air Force get you here. I want to see you on arrival."

"Yes sir. I'll be there as soon as I can."

"No, Paxton. Sooner than that!"

The Director hung up, and Paxton got Pam to work immediately to get him on a plane. He managed to grab a few hours' sleep on the flight, knowing that there might not be much opportunity for rest ahead of him, and arrived at Washington's Reagan National Airport in fairly fresh condition.

A car was waiting for him when he came out of the baggage area, and he was taken to the FBI Building on Pennsylvania Avenue. He was immediately escorted to the office of the Director.

The Director led the way through the outer office, and Paxton could see the secretary reaching for the phone to alert those below to have his car ready at the front door.

They drove in the limousine to the Pentagon, where the driver stopped only briefly at the entrance. It was apparent that the Director's car was well known at this gate.

They marched along the corridors, passing several checkpoints before entering an office complex, to be greeted by two

Marines standing in front of a conference room door. Their credentials were checked one more time, and they passed the saluting sergeant to enter the room, where about a dozen men were seated around a large conference table. Several were in heavily braided uniform.

They took seats side by side near one end of the table, and Paxton took out some papers from his briefcase, placing them on the table in front of him.

At the head of the table was the Chief of National Security. "We can convene the meeting now that the Director has arrived."

"Yes. I'm sorry if we kept you waiting, gentlemen. This is Special Agent in Charge of our Seattle office, George Paxton."

"Very good, Mister Director. Perhaps you could tell the group about the terrorist action in Seattle and the concerns over the more recent events."

"I'll defer to Paxton and let him relate the whole thing, as he has been directly involved from the beginning."

For the next half hour or so, Paxton talked. He told of what had happened at Seatac with the arrival of Sayed Naida and the loss of John Kerrigan. The Fiji connection was described, and he got into the action there at length, explaining the presence of McCann and Eaton as well as accounting for the involvement of Doctor Peter Barclay. There were frequent interruptions with questions from different members of the Commission.

When he got into the involvement of the Fijian police, there was a general stir of disapproval around the table. He spent some time explaining the diplomacy involved in keeping things under a security screen while still managing to pursue the investigation.

"Gentlemen, we've had great cooperation from some of the Fijian security people, but it had to be done surreptitiously. They did great work under cover and lost one of their best men in the process. We were lucky that three more people weren't killed. The Fijians are to be admired, and we owe them a great debt of gratitude—especially for their ability to control the confidentiality of the affair. We had no business entering into an action in their country uninvited, and we could not have managed without them."

"Very good, Paxton, very good," said the Director. "Now continue with your report on the happenings in Fiji which led up to the present situation."

Paxton related the rest of the action in Fiji, including the investigation of the Chinese fishing trawler and the suspicion that the terrorists may have loaded a bomb or other device on the container ship that was heading for Seattle. He finished by telling them that Special Agent Eaton was aboard incognito and was continuing in her efforts to uncover any evidence of a bomb that might be aboard.

"Do you know of any terrorist personnel on the ship?" asked one of the uniformed men seated across the table.

"No sir. We have none identified as yet. There are eight other passengers, and of these there are three who might raise some suspicion. One couple comes from Morocco, and there's a Ph.D. from Tel Aviv University who specializes in Islamic studies. However, we have no evidence that any of the passengers are involved in a plot. The officers and crew have all been aboard since the ship began her voyage in the U.S., and there have been no replacements or additions en route."

The navy brass then spoke up. "Do we have any naval vessels involved in monitoring this ship?" he asked.

He was answered by the Director. "I understand that there's a destroyer now keeping station with the freighter and out of sight of her. But undoubtedly they see each other on radar."

"If there's a chance of a nuclear device on board that ship that's planned to be detonated in Seattle, then we must act," the admiral said. "We must get one of our submarines in position so we can take her out before she reaches the U.S.

coast should your people be unsuccessful in their efforts to find and disarm the weapon."

Paxton was aghast that there was a suggestion of destroying the ship while the passengers and crew were still aboard.

"Sir, I hope that our people can search the containers loaded in Fiji and find the device, if one exists. Should they be successful, then perhaps you could get some expert aboard to disarm it."

"And what if they don't locate it? What then?" asked the admiral quietly. "Do you suggest that we let the ship proceed into L.A. and on to Seattle?"

"Can't we get the people off the ship before you blow it up?" asked Paxton.

"Have you thought that perhaps the terrorists have a means of detonating the bomb remotely?" interjected the army general sitting beside the admiral. "They may even be able to set a delay timer from a remote location."

The talk then opened up around the table. Paxton had to answer many more questions.

The Chief of National Security finally brought the proceedings to a close.

"I'll give my report to the President, and should he need further information from any of you individually, you will be contacted directly. In the meantime it seems expedient that the admiral's initial suggestion is implemented, and he will arrange for one of our submarines to be moved into position close to the *Austral Pioneer* to monitor her activity. For now, however, there will be no effort to interfere with the ship's progress."

The admiral had the last word. "If the FBI can't do the job, then the Navy will."

TWENTY-EIGHT

The Director was not in the best of moods as they drove back to the FBI Building. "What are they doing about searching the containers, Paxton? How are they going to get into them?"

"I guess they're going to need help, sir. I've been thinking about the situation, and I've had only one idea that might give us a way to access the containers boarded in Fiji.

"We've had several occasions when illegal immigrants have been brought to Canada and the West Coast. Some were brought in on fishing boats that were intercepted by the Coast Guard, either Canadian or U.S. But there have been a couple of times recently when they were hidden in containers coming to Seattle. Some of them were D.O.A."

"Yes, I'm familiar with the operation."

"It seemed to me that we could use that as a pretense for a boarding party on the *Austral Pioneer*."

"We've no right to board a foreign vessel on the high seas, and we can't wait for them to get into U.S waters before we search those containers."

"So we have to get the captain to conduct the search for us," said Paxton.

"We inform him that we think there may be illegals being smuggled into the U.S. from Fiji in one of the containers on his ship. If we give him that information, what else can he do but check the Fiji containers himself?"

"But he won't search the containers extensively. He'll just check them for people."

"But now the seals would be off, and our people could then go back later to make another search."

"That might just work, Paxton."

Paxton returned once more to the visiting agents' office and sat thinking about his next move. He could do it in one of two ways. He could contact the captain directly, or he could inform the shipping company and let it direct the captain's actions. The first option seemed better to him. Presented with the possibility of having illegal aliens on his ship, the skipper would have to check the containers that were loaded in Fiji. He must know of the past incidents of illegals being found in containers, including those who arrived dead in Seattle. He would make the search on his own initiative, although he would undoubtedly inform his employers of his actions.

He decided to send the message as a fax and dictated it to a stenographer, who typed it out for him to read and edit. He kept it simple and said only that the FBI had information which indicated the possibility of illegal alien stowaways being in one of the containers that were loaded in Suva. He further indicated that the FBI would board the ship on its arrival in Los Angeles and that the captain's cooperation would be appreciated.

His fax was delivered to the captain as soon as it was received on the *Austral Pioneer*. Captain Watt read it several times.

He called on the intercom to the bridge. "Tell the mate and the chief that I want to see them in my quarters right away."

The order was relayed immediately, and within a few minutes both men were in the captain's cabin.

He handed them the fax, and they read it over before looking back at the captain.

"We'll have to open all the containers loaded in Suva and have a look. There's nothing else we can do," he said. "Obviously it should be done as soon as possible."

After "Happy Hour," the captain came in and walked around the group, greeting people individually or as couples. When he had made the rounds he raised his voice and said, "Ladies and gentlemen, if I could have your attention please, I've a favor to ask of everyone.

"We had a little accident a while ago, and a large container of paint was spilled on the deck. There is no danger involved, but we have to clean it up. I'd appreciate it if you could confine yourselves to the accommodation areas this evening. As I say, there's no safety concern, but things will be messy out there, as we have to use a lot of paint thinner chemicals and then hose it down. I do hope you all understand."

The captain departed soon after making his announcement. Peter and Ann waited several minutes, then they left the lounge and went to see what was going on out on deck.

There were a couple of crewmen with hoses and two more with large brooms who were working along the port side and appeared to be scrubbing vigorously. But they could also see other figures climbing on containers, which Peter thought were those that he and Ann had identified as the ones loaded in Suva. Flashlight beams could be seen in the gloom, though they were well shielded.

They continued to watch as the lights remained in one location for a time and then disappeared for several minutes. The same thing happened in another location, and they realized that the action appeared to be moving from one container to another. The disappearance and reappearance of the lights at the aft end of each one suggested that the containers were each being entered and searched briefly.

"I'll be damned," remarked Peter quietly. "They're searching the Fiji containers for some reason."

"First we'd better wait to hear what Paxton has to say."

They returned to the lounge and had another drink before the group started to break up and head for the dining room.

Peter and Ann sat with the Calverts, Mrs. Kirkpatrick and Dr. Munson. The two round-trippers seemed to be at the same table quite often, which may have been because they were the only unattached individuals.

"How goes your writing, Doctor? You seem to be putting in a lot of time at it," enquired Ann, directing herself to Munson.

"Oh, I'm struggling along with it. It's progressing, but slowly I'm afraid. I've written many articles and papers, but this is my first full book, and the writing seems to be so much more belabored than I had expected it to be."

"I'm sure that's the way with most first books," she commented. "It seems to be a discouraging and at times an overwhelming undertaking for many authors."

"Have you done any writing, Liz?" asked Mrs. Kirkpatrick.

"No. No, I haven't," Ann smiled. "But I've known a few authors, and it seems that with the first book the writing doesn't flow as spontaneously as it does with later efforts."

She turned back to the young Ph.D. "Anyhow, just hang in there and keep plugging along. One of these days you'll get a breakthrough and it'll flow along." She paused and then added with a laugh, " At least that's what they tell me is supposed to happen."

He gave her a grin, and from then on seemed to be more relaxed than they had seen him previously.

"What is the subject of your book, Carroll?" asked Peter. "I know your area of expertise, but I was wondering exactly what you're writing about."

"Well, Simon, I'm glad you're interested. No title yet, but the book is about the Arab-Israeli conflict."

"I'm sure you have a lot to say on the subject too. I know you're an historian, but I trust you'll have something to say about the future as well."

"I'm not sure that I know exactly what you mean, but yes, I certainly have some thoughts on what might happen."

"I was hoping that you intend to express your thoughts on what you think *should* happen, Carroll," said Peter quietly.

Munson stared at him for a few moments before commenting.

"I do intend to do just that, Simon, but one can only express one's opinion on the matter. It's very complicated, and no one knows all the answers, although some seem to think they do."

"Do you think there's a hope for peace in the region?" asked Ann.

He looked thoughtful for a moment or two before answering.

"I think there will be temporary periods without violence. But a lasting peace? No. I can't see it. No more so than in Northern Ireland or Eastern Europe or in different areas throughout Africa, Asia and the Americas. Ethnic, religious and economic differences will prevent permanent settlement of disputes in these regions."

"You paint a bleak picture," answered Ann. "But it's hard to disagree with you."

"Getting back to the Middle East," said Peter and then paused briefly before going on. "Will your book show that you side with the Arabs or with the Jews?"

Munson smiled.

"I hope that I come out looking relatively unbiased, my friend. But you will have to read the book and make up your own mind about that," he said with a laugh.

"I'll look forward to it," Peter said.

The main course came. A baked ham with raisin sauce. Professor Calvert called the waiter over and asked if they could have vegetarian plates.

"That's funny," joked Dr. Munson. "You don't look Jewish."

The Calverts were not amused. Peter changed the subject, and soon they were talking about his beloved Fiji. This went on until Ann said to Peter, "We should get up to the bridge pretty soon. I promised Dad I'd call him tonight, but I don't want to leave it too late."

"Oh yes, okay." He turned to their table partners. "Please excuse us. We'll join you later for coffee in the lounge."

They went up to the bridge to find the First Officer on watch.

Looking forward over the stack of containers, Peter said, "All looks quiet out there. The big cleanup is over and done with, I assume."

"Oh, yes sir. All taken care of."

Peter looked forward again. He was glad to see there were no lights shining in the direction of the Fijian containers.

They went in and placed another phone call. Ann dialed the number and after a moment or two could hear the ringing tones, and then Paxton answered with a gruff "Yes?"

"Hello, Dad," she greeted him. "How are you tonight?"

"I'm just great, my dear. How are things with you? Are you still enjoying your voyage?"

"You bet. Simon and I are having a very relaxing time and enjoying every moment. We're just wondering if we're supposed to talk with the captain if we're worried about arriving late or anything."

"Only if you're really not doing well. Otherwise, the captain has other concerns."

"Thanks, Dad," Agent Eaton went on.

"That's okay, dear. Like I've always said, have fun and don't be distracted by what may be below the surface."

Ann hung up the phone and turned to Peter. "Let's get on with this. You have to know that there's no way Uncle Sam is going to let this bomb reach the U.S. One way or another they're going to stop it. The boss says, 'Don't be distracted by what's below the surface.' He's telling me they have a submarine shadowing us as their insurance.

"We can't make our move until the wee hours," she continued. "Now let's go down to the lounge and put in our usual after dinner appearance for coffee. We don't want to do anything out of the ordinary just now. Later tonight we'll sneak down to try to get a look into those containers."

They left the bridge and went down to the lounge, where they found the other passengers having tea, coffee and after dinner drinks. The Marquands, Munson and Mrs. Kirkpatrick were having port. The Calverts only had coffee. The talk was light and the time late. Peter and Ann left after an hour.

When they got back to their room, there was the usual tension about getting into bed.

"This is getting ridiculous, Ann. I know you're working the case, but…"

"That won't last forever, Peter," she said. "Pleasant dreams."

Peter tossed and turned. Ann didn't sleep at all. She nudged him a little after two. A heavy cloud had obscured the moon, and it was quite dark out.

They dressed in the darkest clothing they had and left the stateroom. Closing the door quietly, they slipped along the corridor and down the stairs to get out on deck on the port side. Holding tightly along the sides of the containers at deck level, they got to the area where they had seen the Fiji containers, and Ann climbed up to get to the second tier to take an exploratory look. She was down again in a few minutes.

"What's the matter?" Peter whispered. "Why did you come back down so quickly?"

"We can't do it. We can't get into them," she answered quietly.

"Why not? Didn't they remove the seals?"

"Yes, they did. But then they replaced them with chains and padlocks!"

TWENTY-NINE

In the morning they went to see the captain. It was a last resort.

They found the captain sitting with the chief.

"Sorry to bother you, captain, but we need to talk with you," said Agent Eaton.

"But of course," answered the Englishman in his usual gracious manner. "Nothing wrong I hope?"

"Would you like me to leave?" interjected the chief, standing up as he spoke.

"No chief, I think you ought to stay," answered Peter. "This will be of concern to you also."

The captain got up and pulled out two more chairs from the table.

"Please sit down. Now what can I do for you?"

Peter asked, "Do you mind if I close the door?"

Watt gestured towards the door, and Peter walked over to close it before joining the others at the table.

"This is beginning to look ominous," said the captain. "I'm afraid I may not like what I'm about to hear."

"I'm on a mission for the United States government," Ann announced abruptly. "The doctor is assisting me."

"I knew I wasn't going to like this," said Watt. "Go on."

Peter and Ann spent the next half hour telling the story of terrorists in Seattle and Fiji and explaining their reasons for believing there might be a nuclear weapon on the *Austral Pioneer*.

"That's why I got the fax that got us to take a look in the containers loaded in Fiji," the Captain said.

Ann nodded. "We had to get you to remove the seals so we could later search them for the device. But you stymied us when you chained and locked them. That's why we have to ask for your help now."

"And what if we refuse to become involved?"

"Captain, you're already involved. We're asking for your help, and also your discretion. Gentlemen, we believe it's quite possible that there's a terrorist agent or agents on board. It may be that there's more than one, and we don't know if they might be among the passengers or in the crew—possibly both."

The chief spoke up then. "I can't believe that a threat of this magnitude is being left in your hands alone. What else is being done to protect the U.S. from this menace?"

"I've not been informed of what other measures are planned," said Ann. "But I think there's little doubt that this ship is being shadowed by the U.S. Navy. It would be my guess that if we can't come up with some answers before we approach the West Coast, then they may choose to sink the *Austral Pioneer* while she's still well out in the Pacific."

Both men looked astounded.

"Surely you realize what a catastrophe would result should a nuclear device be detonated in Seattle," Peter said.

"What do you want us to do?" the captain asked.

"First let us impress upon both of you the need for secrecy. We don't know who the enemy is on board, but we have to assume that there is at least one. We have to act covertly at all times. You both understand the necessity for this? We need you to help us get into the containers that you have already unsealed. We'll have to do it during the night I suppose."

"What about the terrorists aboard?" asked the chief. "Do you have any suspects?"

"Not really," answered Ann. "The background of a couple of the passengers is suggestive. Dr. Munson has been in Islamic studies for many years and lives and works in Israel where there are many Islamic extremists. Similarly, the Marquands are from the part of North Africa where many countries harbor terrorists. We know nothing about your crew. Do either of you have any suspicions regarding possible terrorists among the seamen or engine room staff?"

Each shook his head.

"We would have discussed such a thing in our morning session if it had come to light," Watt said. "Nothing like this has ever come up."

"You haven't heard any talk aboard that would lead you to suspect that someone has extremist views? I mean either within the crew or amongst the passengers?" she persisted.

"Nothing at all."

"Well, we'll have to keep a close eye on everyone in that case. Do you have any side arms on board?"

"Yes," answered the captain. "I've a couple of Army revolvers, which are kept locked away in the captain's safe."

"Okay. You'd better get them out and check them over. I hope you both know how to use them if it becomes necessary."

They both looked startled, and she realized that neither man had contemplated that kind of involvement.

"We'd better get down to breakfast before we're missed and someone gets suspicious," suggested Peter.

Ann nodded. "I'll be calling my superior and I'll let you know if there's anything new. What time do you suggest we make our container inspection?"

"I'd guess two o'clock in the morning would be a good hour," Captain Watt said. "That's half way through the middle watch, and there are no scheduled rounds at that time. But there is something that clearly you haven't thought about with regard to searching the containers."

"And what's that, captain?"

"You should realize that most of them are crammed full."

Peter turned to look at the captain and said, "We have a Geiger counter to help us locate a nuclear device. Maybe you could provide a pole of some kind to allow us to probe with it through the length of a container?"

"We'll do what we can for you," the captain said, looking at the chief, who nodded.

They rose to leave and then, in parting, Watt said, "Don't let them sink my ship."

"Only as a last resort, captain," answered Ann. "Only as a last resort."

They descended to the officer's mess for breakfast and found all the other passengers there except for Dr. Munson who, as usual, was skipping breakfast and presumably was working on his book.

Mid morning found them back in the communications center on the bridge, where Ann put through a call to Paxton. He now had them on a secure line.

They told him about the developments that had resulted in their drafting of the captain and the chief into the operation. Paxton expressed his apprehension, but understood the necessity for the move.

"How did they respond?" he asked.

"They were shocked, of course," answered Ann. "But they're sensible men and took things quite well, considering." She paused. "The captain is very concerned that we might have to sink his ship."

"I hope we can find a way to avoid doing that," responded Paxton. "The sinking of a ship belonging to a friendly foreign nation by the U.S. Navy would create a tremendous anti American response throughout the world no matter what the reason for the action."

Ann said, "Yes sir, everyone would agree with you on that."

"We've had some action from your friends in Fiji," continued Paxton.

"Tukana called from Nadi Airport. Seems they'd followed Saliheen and Aziz from Suva and managed to stick with them without being spotted. They watched them check in on the Air Pacific flight that left last night for LAX. We alerted the L.A. office, and they'll have a bunch of agents waiting for them when they land. We don't want to pick them up yet. It's better that we find out where they're going first. Our guess, of course, is that they're heading for Seattle. Anyhow, their work in Fiji appears to be finished."

"That'll be a relief to Tukana, but even more so to Kabuta," Ann said. "Maybe these two will lead you to the group in Seattle."

"That's what we're hoping for, obviously. We'll have a large number of people involved in the surveillance once the plane lands at LAX. We don't intend to lose them or scare them off."

"Their airline booking was only to L.A. and not beyond?"

"Correct. We have no idea where they'll go from there. Maybe they'll head for Seattle. Maybe they'll hang around L.A. waiting for the arrival of the *Austral Pioneer*. At this point we just don't know."

"Is our unseen colleague now in position?" asked Ann.

"Yes, she arrived there late yesterday and will be with you at least until you reach the coast."

"We hope we don't have to call on her," commented Peter.

"We all hope she won't be needed. The biggest threat there is that some of the powers that be in this operation might go off half cocked and throw her into action."

There was a long pause as they digested this thought.

"How's McCann doing?" asked Peter.

"As petulant as ever," answered Paxton. "He has taken on the Tilbury slaying as a personal crusade."

"Give him our regards."

"I'll do that. Call me when you've inspected those containers."

A rainsquall had descended on the ship, and they went to the lounge to find a number of the other passengers already present, some reading and others playing cards or chatting.

They found seats next to the Marquands, which was fortuitous, as they had wanted to get to know more about the couple from Morocco. They had to try to establish a rapport with the teacher and his wife to learn more about them. In particular they needed to get information on their political leanings, if any. This meant probing to generate a reaction. But it had to be done delicately in order to avoid raising suspicion.

The two men talked about travel and discussed their recent visits to Australia. The women were discussing fashion, but Ann had one ear tuned to the other conversation. She was more concerned with where Peter was going with the men's talk.

He found an opening after Marquand brought up something about the Aborigines and their relationships with the whites in Australia.

"The ethnic problems in your part of the world seem to have settled down in the last few years," said Peter.

"Only in some areas," answered Marquand. "Things have been quieter in Morocco now that the freedom fighters are no longer fighting the French. However, there are still insurrections from time to time. The communists are still active, and there are other extremist groups who erupt into action and cause death and mayhem."

"How about Islamic extremists?" asked Peter. "Are they active in Morocco?"

The question caused Marquand to turn his head and face Peter with a glare.

"The Moroccan people support the Arab cause and, of course, they're behind the Palestinians, if that is what you're asking."

"Well, the Islamic extremists in Algeria have caused many horrible deaths of innocent people, and there have been atrocities in Egypt too. It must be upsetting that Gaddafi provides a training ground for terrorists next door to you in Libya."

"Now we're back to semantics," Marquand sneered. "What some call terrorists, others see as freedom fighters. This always seems to come up when an abused people are struggling to break out from under the yoke of oppression. Why can't the Americans acknowledge the rights of the Arab people and stop being so one-sided, always supporting the Jews?"

"I don't think they're all that one-sided." Peter said. "There have been many occasions when they've put a check on Israeli aggression."

"Oh really," said Marquand sarcastically. "I don't recall too many such occasions, and I believe their support on the side of the Palestinians has been minimal."

"I didn't mean to upset you, and I apologize if I've done so."

"It is I who should apologize," Marquand responded, backtracking. "I tend to get a little carried away on this subject."

"How did you get into supporting the Arab cause so vehemently when you have a French background?" asked Peter, adding, "I hope you don't mind me asking?"

"No, I don't mind your question, Simon. It seems a natural one, as the Arabs were besetting the French when my father worked in Morocco before and after independence. The simple fact is, I was influenced strongly to believe in the cause of the local people from the time I went to school in Morocco before taking up my college education in France. I never forgot the cause and have continued to support it since returning to live and work there."

"I can understand that."

Ann was thinking, *Mark up another possible suspect!*

THIRTY

The rest of the day remained overcast after the rainstorm had passed, and they spent it indoors, mostly reading and working on crossword puzzles.

At the cocktail gathering they had a moment alone with the chief, who told them he had prepared a pole that could be extended in sections, allowing them to reach into the containers at different depths.

"That should work just fine, Chief," said Ann. "The Geiger counter is small. It's a digital handheld job and doesn't weigh much. I just hope we can reach it far enough into the containers to search them adequately."

"We'll see," said the chief. "Access will vary according to how tightly they're packed. But there's a good chance that what you're looking for might have been loaded last into one of the boxes. In that case it would be near the front, closer to the door."

They had dinner that evening with their traveling group. The cook had prepared a seafood scampi, which everyone enjoyed. There was plenty of wine to go around, as Mrs. Kirkpatrick and the Calverts had none. Ann only sipped hers.

After dinner they spent an hour or so in the lounge, then Peter and Ann went to their stateroom, where they laid out their clothes and the bag of gear for the night outing. Peter set his wristwatch alarm.

At one thirty a.m. they left the cabin and quietly descended to the deck on the port side, as they had done on the previous night. They edged along the side of the containers till they reached those loaded in Fiji, where they had to climb up to the second tier. This was made easier for them by a knotted rope was hanging down from above, courtesy of the chief, who was already waiting at the second tier level with the captain.

"We thought we'd start at this level first," the chief whispered, and then he turned to the nearest container to open the padlock and undo the chain securing the door. Next he taped the Geiger counter to one end of a section of the extension pole.

The first four containers were full to the door, and at first they thought they would not be able to access each chamber. But with the door closed they were able to use flashlights and found slots between the various items, enabling them to move the pole-mounted Geiger counter so it reached all the way to the back wall. Nothing registered in the first four. They were free of radiation.

The fifth container was not as full as the others. They found free space at the front when they entered. After closing the door, they turned on their flashlights.

Near the front of the load was a large oblong wooden crate, and when Peter hit the switch on the Geiger counter, it immediately emitted a rapid clicking sound.

"My God!" exclaimed the captain.

"Jesus!" the chief said, awe in his voice, "it's radioactive!"

Peter moved the instrument back and forth, towards and then away from the crate. The clicking noise increased in rate and intensity the closer it got to the wooden coffin-like structure. "It sure looks that way," he said quietly. "Let's just run this thing around the rest of this container to see if anything else shows up 'hot.'"

They made a thorough scan of the rest of the chamber, but the clicking came only from the oblong wooden box.

"What do we do now?" asked the captain.

"We have to get a look inside this crate," said Ann. "But we can't take a chance on opening it ourselves. It could be booby-trapped."

She looked at the three men. "We need some help at this stage. Gentlemen, I believe it's time to call in some experts. Under no circumstances is this container to be touched by anyone else."

No one gave her any argument.

"I'm going to call my chief. But I think that the other containers have to be inspected also just to rule them out."

"Okay, Ann," Peter said. "We'll carry on with the search and when we've finished we'll meet you in the captain's cabin for a chat." Turning to Watt, he added, "If that's okay with you, sir?"

"Yes, of course," answered the skipper, who was not about to argue.

The men continued with their search, examining the other three non-refrigerated containers with no further response from the Geiger counter. They secured each of the container doors with the chains and padlocks as before.

When they reached the captain's cabin, they found Ann was already there waiting for them.

"What's the word?" asked Peter as they walked in.

"Apparently they had already set up the next move contingent on us coming up with a positive finding with the Geiger counter," she answered. "Paxton is signaling a destroyer that's been shadowing us, and there should be a Navy Seals team already on their way by now. We may not have much time," she said, tension in her voice. "Remember, we don't know the terrorists' schedule." The captain nodded glumly.

She looked at Peter. "You and I are to maintain our cover and continue trying to identify the agent or agents on aboard. We'll have to leave it to the captain and the chief to greet the visitors. They'll take over the packing case and its contents. What they find could be the deciding factor in the equation on what comes next."

THIRTY-ONE

The twin engine SH60 Seahawk arrived over the *Austral Pioneer,* and in the early dawn light they could see it lower itself over the containers in the forward deck area. As they watched from the bridge, it hovered over the upper tier of containers, and three figures were seen jumping out, followed by some bags that were tossed down to them. The helicopter then lifted off again, and the noise receded as it slipped sideways to disappear into the gloom.

The captain and the chief went down to the main deck level and ran forward to greet the new arrivals.

"Good morning," one of the dark clad men called down.

"Yes, good morning. I'm Captain Desmond Watt, and this is my Chief Engineer, Cameron Hill."

"We're the bomb disposal team from the destroyer that's been keeping an eye on you. I'm Lieutenant Commander Brand with Chiefs Denison and Hatton."

Hill's knotted rope was still in position, and the two climbed up to join the Navy men on the second tier. They all shook hands, and then the captain led the way to the container that held the radioactive crate.

"This way, gentlemen." He stepped forward to open the padlock and undo the chain. The newcomers brought their bags in with them, and as soon as the door was closed, the chief turned on his flashlight, directing its beam towards the radioactive crate.

"This is the one," he said.

The group leader signaled his team to scan the container. It emitted rapid clicking sounds.

The Navy men now inspected the outside surface of the crate under a halogen light, and then ran around it with a metal detector. The leader used it like a stud finder on a wall. When he was satisfied with the location of the crate fasteners, he used a hand drill to make a hole in the side of the crate at the top edge near the lid. He inserted a flexible lighted scope gently into the hole and began an examination of the inside.

After a ten-minute search with the scope, he announced there were no indications of a booby trap. He had managed to access the upper section and felt confident the lid could be safely removed. They then used tools to pry the lid loose all the way around its circumference. It was gently lifted free and placed aside.

All five men gathered around the wooden crate to look inside. They saw a cylinder with a dull metallic finish that was about two meters in length and a half-meter in diameter. It had some writing on the casing in Chinese characters. There were three plates, one large and two small ones, along the upper surface that were secured with slotted screws. The device was held in place in a wooden rack within the crate.

"Well, there she is, guys," exclaimed the team leader. "This is a nuke. Old, but that doesn't lessen the threat."

"Can you tell if it's set to go off?" asked Watt.

"There's no way to be sure without taking off the faceplate and looking inside," answered the team leader. "This type doesn't have setting controls on the outside of the casing but, as you can see, the l.e.d.'s are not illuminated."

"Can you disarm it?" asked Hill, his voice cracking.

"I certainly hope so, but first we have to get the plate off without setting off any surprises."

"You mean they may have set a booby trap for that maneuver?"

Brand applied the blade of the screwdriver to the first of the securing screws on the largest of the three faceplates. He applied some counterclockwise force and eventually felt the screw begin to turn. He left the first screw and moved to one diagonally opposite to loosen it slightly. Then he continued to partially loosen the other screws around the faceplate until he knew that they were all extractable. He then began removing the screws one by one until only two diagonally opposite screws held the faceplate. As he undid the last two he used them to hold the plate as he eased it off the weapons casing.

He finally stood back and stretched his shoulders. "It's armed, but the timer hasn't been set as far as I can tell," he said eventually.

"Can you disarm it, and would that make it inactive and safe?" asked the captain.

"I believe I can and, yes, it would then be in a dormant state."

"Meaning that if someone were to set the timer thereafter, it would not explode?"

"It can be disabled in that way. But why do you ask?"

"There may well be a terrorist on my ship. Wouldn't it be a good idea to fix the bomb so that if he were to get to it and set the timer, it wouldn't go off?"

Brand thought about this for a few moments. "Makes sense to me, Captain. Let me see what I can do with it."

"One other question," added Watt. "Would he be able to set the timer remotely—I mean without having to remove the faceplate?"

"That's exactly how he would do it, Captain. But, of course, he would need the appropriate equipment to be able to do so."

THIRTY-TWO

Paxton was more impatient now that things were finally happening. The Seattle A. I. C. was not the only one.

The moment he got the word that Saliheen and Aziz were on their way from Fiji, McCann wanted to hop on the first available flight to L.A. Paxton pointed out that they knew him and could recognize him if they saw him.

"Okay," said McCann. "But if you lose them, you're gonna need me 'cause I'm the only one around here who knows them by sight."

Aziz and Saliheen got off the aircraft separately, and it was fortunate that there were enough agents to cover them. They both cleared immigration and customs without delay. Once outside the terminal building they went their separate ways, Aziz to the left, carrying a duffel bag, and Saliheen to the right, pulling along a wheeled suitcase.

Saliheen boarded the interairline bus that circled the airport and was seen to dismount at Terminal 7, where he went to the United Airlines ticket counter. After he left, the ticket agent was questioned by one of the FBI team, who then transmitted the information to the others that their man was booked on a flight to Seattle leaving in thirty minutes from gate number twenty-eight. Two more seats, situated close to the terrorist, were quickly requisitioned on the same flight, and unbeknownst to Saliheen, there were several people in the crowd at the gate who had more than a passing interest in his movements.

Aziz walked around the airport from the International Terminal in a counterclockwise direction to the adjacent Terminal 3. He was followed to the Alaska Airlines desk where he booked on a flight to Seattle. It was arranged that he too was to be in the anonymous company of some of Uncle Sam's employees during his trip.

The two flights arrived at Seatac at about the same time. Paxton had people in position at the arrival gates and baggage areas serving both. The local men, combined with the L.A. agents who had accompanied them on the aircraft, had the two Pakistanis well covered.

Saliheen took a hotel bus to the Evergreen Airport Hotel, a mile away from Seatac. The agents, who watched as he checked in, saw he was registered in room 331. They acquired room 333. They installed listening equipment on the phone line and the wall.

Aziz took a cab to a different local airport hotel, the Blackhawk Seatac. He was booked into room 245, and the agents set up shop next door.

Paxton received reports from the men watching the Pakistanis and expected to learn more through the phone monitoring. But all was quiet during the rest of the day, and he guessed that both men might be catching up on their sleep.

Paxton received a call from Ann Eaton bringing him up to date on the action aboard the *Austral Pioneer*. She told him about the Navy Seals team and their findings on the bomb.

"It's in a safe mode now," she said. "But obviously we're not out of the woods yet. We still haven't identified the terrorist who might be aboard."

"Did the Navy guys leave yet?" he asked.

"No, they're still in the container. They're planning for a pickup tonight, probably about two a.m."

"Do you know how many of the Fiji containers are to be unloaded in Los Angeles?"

"We don't have any idea, but we'll be waiting anxiously to see which ones go ashore there. It's a pretty safe bet that the bomb is headed for Seattle, don't you think?"

"Everything points that way. But there's still a chance they might send it by surface up the coast, either road or rail."

"If there's a terrorist on this ship, then I'd guess that the weapon would stay aboard with him."

"You're probably right on that. Anyhow, keep me informed."

He told her about the arrival of the two men from Fiji and assured her they were being closely watched.

"We're waiting for them to lead us to the other members of the group that killed the Seattle cop," he said. "I hope we get to them before McCann does. He's got blood in his eye."

"You're right, let's hope he doesn't get too carried away. He feels owed for Vijay Dass and Mary Tilbury as well as for Tukana and himself."

After finishing her call with Paxton, Ann went with Peter to the captain's cabin, where they had a meeting.

"We do have to make sure we don't have a bad guy aboard," Ann Eaton said. "If they've a remote detonator, the whole ship could go up."

"We can hardly search everyone's stateroom and all their belongings," the captain protested. "Besides, the thing could be hidden so well we might never find it. It could even be disguised as something else—like a portable radio, a tape player or a laptop. Who knows?"

"Maybe they'll give themselves away," Peter said. "We'll keep at it."

That night the helicopter came in to hover briefly and thirty seconds later was on its way again, with the navy team safely aboard.

The *Austral Pioneer* steamed into San Pedro Harbor shepherded by three tugs. Brought alongside at a containership wharf, she was tied up and the engine was shut down for the first time in twelve days. Unloading began as soon as the ship had been secured, and the noise picked up as the cranes and trucks went to work. None of the passengers went ashore, as there was nothing to attract them locally during the short stay.

Containers were soon being hauled up and swung over the side to be deposited onto trucks and trailers that moved along in a continuous column.

The captain was informed that some five hundred and twenty containers were to be unloaded, and the rest were to continue on to Seattle. He was not given any details regarding which ones were to be taken off.

Peter and Ann observed when cranes approached the boxes loaded in Fiji. They watched as the containers were hooked up to the crane. Most were off loaded, but not the one containing the bomb.

After the tugs had cast loose, the *Austral Pioneer* headed out to sea, and eventually her bow turned north, heading for Seattle with the bomb still aboard.

THIRTY-THREE

Paxton's impatience continued to increase as the time passed without anything being heard by the agents watching the two Pakistanis. However, after about six hours of silence, the agents in the next room could hear Saliheen moving around, and then he picked up the phone to make a call. The telephone number and the conversation were both recorded on the FBI equipment.

After the number called had rung several times, the phone was picked up.

The conversation was in English, and it was apparent that the speakers did not share a native language.

"Yes?"

"We are here," said Saliheen.

"At the place where you planned to be?"

"Yes, and my colleague should be at his agreed upon location also."

"We will pick you up out in front of your hotel in thirty minutes, and then we will get your friend. Let him know."

The connection broke.

Saliheen then made a call to Aziz at the Blackhawk. The agents did not understand Urdu.

Cars were posted near the exit from the Evergreen, and when Saliheen drove away in a gray Nissan, they followed.

The Nissan turned into the entrance of the Blackhawk.

After collecting Aziz from outside his hotel, the gray car turned south on Highway 99 with yet another FBI vehicle pulling out and falling in line at a three-car distance behind.

They continued south to Federal Way, where the Nissan turned off to the right, the two following cars still behind.

Eventually the Nissan turned into a trailer park, and the lead pursuit vehicle continued past the entrance to stop further along the road. The other FBI cars also stopped near the trailer park and established a perimeter. They watched as their quarry went into a large trailer and shortly emerged with two others. One car stayed behind to survey the trailer, and the pursuit back to the hotels was completed.

The chase cars brought video back to Paxton. Paxton did not know the two new bad guys, but he had his suspicions. These were confirmed when he e-mailed the video to McCann.

"Print these up and get copies to McCann at S.P.D. right away," ordered Paxton. "I'll let him know you'll be there shortly."

When McCann got the word, he informed Mat Benson, who then told Coulter and Patterson to stand by for a run down to Renton for another visit with the widow Doyle. He told them they were to show her the pictures and see if she could identify the two men from the trailer in Federal Way as her recent neighbors.

Mrs. Doyle confirmed the identification. She was sure that the men were two of the three who had lived across the street.

After the two detectives reported in, McCann called Paxton.

"The two guys in the photos from Federal Way are the same ones who lived in the Renton house," McCann reported. "I hope your guys are keeping a real close eye on that trailer, Director Paxton. We still haven't seen any sign of Naida. He's the sonofabitch that I want. For Kerrigan."

"Don't worry, Mac, I promise you we'll get him. For what it's worth, I don't think he'll make a move till the ship arrives in Seattle."

The *Austral Pioneer* made good time up the coast and proceeded in an easterly direction towards Port Angeles. She slowed to take the pilot on board.

The helmsman was now taking directions from the pilot, although the captain remained in command of the ship.

After passing Point Wilson, the course was altered to the southeast, and the *Austral Pioneer* went through Admiralty Inlet to enter Puget Sound, passing a panorama of the Olympic Mountains to the west and Mount Baker to the east.

As they approached Seattle's Elliott Bay, Mount Rainier was seen standing out in all its glory in the evening sunshine and was likened by Mrs. Kirkpatrick to a big ice-cream cone.

Ann was commenting on the beauty of the scene.

"Early September is often the best time to see it," said Peter. "It's called Indian Summer."

The ship was now moving slowly, as she was joined by two tugs to which towlines were made fast, fore and aft. They gently eased her alongside at one of the container ship berths at Terminal 18.

Watching from a car positioned behind some wharf sheds were Paxton and McCann. McCann had binoculars trained on the ship, and eventually he spotted Peter and Ann looking down from the "D" deck level on the starboard side.

As it was getting late in the day when the ship was finally secured, none of the passengers was planning to disembark until the next morning. Peter and Ann also remained aboard.

The unloading was not to begin until daylight, but vehicles were entering and leaving the dock during the evening to service and supply the ship before the onset of the heavy truck traffic in the morning would limit access.

Ann put her hand on Peter's arm as they were about to enter the Farewell Dinner party. "We are no closer to uncovering a hidden terrorist aboard than we were when we started the trip in Suva. We'll have to keep an eye on everyone tonight and look out for someone making a move to head out. Sooner or later, our suspect has to make a move towards the container to set the timer."

"I've been thinking of something else," said Peter. "The Navy guys have fixed the weapon so the trigger setting device won't activate the timer, but isn't it likely that the readout on his device will inform him of that? In other words, he'll know that he was unsuccessful in the remote activation process."

"You mean he or someone else who has the knowledge would have to set the weapon manually?"

"Precisely. Then somebody with enough knowledge will set it to go off immediately, with no timed delay. A suicide bombing, and everyone in this part of the Northwest would die with him."

They had reached the lounge.

"The drinks are on me," Larry Johnson said as they entered. "Everybody has to have a good time 'cause this is our last night together."

Everyone was there, and all seemed to be having a good time, the Johnsons, the Calverts, the Marquands, Munson and Mrs. Kirkpatrick.

Professor Munson was the first to leave. Ann left to follow him briefly, then returned to rejoin the others.

The party continued for another hour or so before people began to leave. Peter and Ann went slowly to their cabin, chatting with the other passengers as they made their way along and observing them entering their various cabins. They changed into the dark clothing they had worn on their previous night prowl. They left the cabin and went down to the main deck to approach the Fiji containers.

"Don't move, Doctor, Mrs. Armour," said a familiar voice from behind. "There are pistols pointed at the back of your heads."

"Why Professor and Mrs. Calvert, you surprise us," said Ann. She was turning ever so slightly so that she could draw her weapon.

Professor Calvert nudged Peter's skull with the gun muzzle. "Today the world will see the greatest blow to the American 'Great Satan' that Islam has ever achieved, and we have been chosen to be Allah's instrument of vengeance."

"How did you get involved in this?" Ann persisted.

"We converted to Islam when I was a visiting professor in Beirut many years ago. We have been in deep cover ever since, awaiting the call to serve Allah," announced Calvert proudly.

While Mrs. Calvert kept them covered, he disarmed Peter and tied their hands behind their backs.

"And now what, Professor?" asked Ann. "Where do we go from here?"

"I suspect you will go to meet your Christian god. As we speak, I am setting the timer."

Silence hung in the air. Then Calvert whispered to his wife, "I can't get it to register the correct activation response. Something's wrong. It appears to be unable to set the trigger."

"We can't stay around here much longer," she hissed. "You'll have to call them on the cell phone." She handed over the phone from the same bag that had contained the unsuccessful triggering device, and he called a cell phone number that was answered immediately.

He explained that the setting routine was not producing the desired results on the readout and listened for a while.

"I've already tried all that," he said exasperatedly. "Nothing seems to work."

After listening again, he said, "Very well, but you better hurry. Somebody's going to catch on pretty soon. We can't wait around here forever."

He ended the call and told his wife, "We have to get into the container with these two and stay there until the others arrive. The weapon will have to be set manually."

She looked frightened. "You make it sound like we are not going to have time to get away. Is that how it's going to be?"

"We always knew that would be a strong possibility, and circumstances are starting to move against us now, my dear."

It was obvious they had come well prepared. Calvert pushed Ann forward and, using a bolt cutter from the bag, cut through the chain on the door of the container.

He opened the container door far enough to allow them access one at a time, and they went inside with the pistols held on the captives.

"Sit on the floor," he ordered. Peter and Ann sat down.

A call to Saliheen mobilized the FBI agents. They followed as Saliheen and Aziz were picked up in the gray Nissan, which then headed to the docks.

The terrorists parked across the street under the Alaska Way Viaduct. As they approached the terminal gate, a Bureau SWAT team was waiting for them.

Two FBI cars came screaming through the outer gate of the wharf, and as the four men turned to face them, they heard a shout from behind, ordering them to drop their weapons or be killed. The SWAT team rushed out of the hut.

Saliheen made the mistake of raising his weapon. He was immediately gunned down. The FBI agents moved forward as the other three terrorists threw away their weapons.

An electrician's van parked inside the terminal. Carrying a toolbox, Sayed Naida hurried up the gangplank and turned back along the bank of containers to get to the one containing the bomb.

He entered through the partially open door to find the Calverts standing inside alongside Peter and Ann, who were on the floor, their wrists secured behind their backs.

"Good work. You've done your job well."

"But we couldn't get the timer programmed with the activator," said Calvert. "I don't know what's wrong with it."

"At this stage, it isn't going to matter. You see it's too late for a timer now."

"He means he's going to detonate the bomb now," said Peter. "There will be no timer delay."

"Very good, Doctor," said Naida. "You get top marks for figuring that out, now don't you."

When the gunshots were heard from the gate area, Naida turned back to listen. "Now the urgency has moved up a notch." Turning to his bag, he took out tools to start undoing the screws on the faceplate of the bomb. Ann took the opportunity to show Peter the .32 automatic strapped to her ankle.

"I won't let you do it," suddenly erupted Calvert. "You can't kill Maria. We were promised a chance to get away before the bomb detonated. You can't do this."

Suddenly he grabbed Naida by the shoulder and pulled him around. The swarthy terrorist snarled and, reaching for Maria's arm, snatched her pistol and then, holding it against the side of her head, pulled the trigger.

"There," he growled. "Now there will be no more trouble with that problem."

Calvert let out a cry and dropped to his knees beside his dead wife on the ground.

Naida worked to remove the screws and suddenly, Calvert shouted, "You evil bastard," and turned his pistol towards the Arab. But Naida was too quick for him and plunged his screwdriver into the professor's eye socket before the old man could get off a shot. He joined his wife on the floor as Ann and Peter looked on in horrified silence.

As Naida returned to his task, Peter moved quietly to grab the tiny automatic from Ann's ankle with his tied hands.

"This will all be over soon," Naida said, "A glorious blow to the infidels and a glorious gift to..."

Dr. Peter Barclay fired five shots from the tiny automatic. The first and third hollow point rounds did their job, and Naida was dead.

In moments a dozen FBI agents were upon them. Peter and Ann were taken out on deck.

"That's the first time I killed anybody," said the shaken Peter.

"And the last time."

"Right, that's your job, Agent Eaton."

"Not anymore, Peter. The only thing I'm thinking about is a long vacation. Maybe a permanent one."

"And where would that be?"

"Why in Fiji, of course, Dr. Barclay. On the lovely island of Viti Levu."

EPILOGUE

The *Noqui Tau* was tied up at the float by the villa as usual, but she certainly did not have her usual appearance.

The ladies of the neighborhood had been very busy since daybreak, and with the help of Jone and Ramesh, they had transformed the cruiser, which was now bedecked with flowers and bunting of many colors. Across the transom was a large sign that said, "Just Married."

At the church the choir were singing lustily, and the wedding guests also were belting out the well-known hymns. It was obviously going to be a wedding to remember, if the start of the proceedings was any indication of things to come.

Peter stood at the front of the church, and by his side were Dan Tukana and Craig Kendall. He looked back at the pews and saw most all of the people who had been such a close part of his life in Fiji.

Isiloni Kabuta stood beside his wife, and alongside her was Kendall's wife.

Mere and her husband were with Jone and Ramesh, and she was smiling all the while.

Even old Ratu Timoci had put in an appearance and was being shepherded by his son, Phillip Kavoka.

The introductory hymn finally ended, and the organist struck up the familiar strains of the Wedding March.

Everyone turned to face the back of the church in expectation, and at the door the bridal party appeared. The bridesmaids, Sarita Chand, followed by Salote Turuva, each wearing a blue trimmed white dress and a blue hat and carrying a posy of white gardenias, led the procession.

The bride, Ann Eaton, was looking radiant, as would be expected. She was dressed in a short white wedding dress with blue trim and carried a bouquet of blue gardenias. Walking beside her was Gerry McCann, who was dressed in long white pants and a flowered shirt with a garland of flowers hanging around his neck.

As they reached the altar and turned to face the guests, Kabuta looked at them, thinking what a lot of trouble they had caused him, but feeling very proud of all of them and what they had achieved. His eyes dimmed for a moment as he thought of Vijay Dass, wishing he could have been with them. He pictured Vijay's spirit looking down at the gathering and smiling with approval.

The ceremony proceeded with considerable pomp, and the reverend conducting it seemed to delight in promoting its importance as well as his own.

The reception was at the villa, and there was a large tanoa of yaqona, alongside which Ratu Timoci deposited himself for the afternoon. In addition, the beer and wine flowed copiously, accompanied by liberal quantities of rum drinks of various flavors.

"Who'd a thought we'd have been here and still all in one piece after everything we went through together?" commented McCann to Peter as they stood together enjoying a couple of cold stubbies.

"It was quite a ride that we all took since you first arrived here, Mac," said Peter. "Too bad that old Dass didn't make it to this shindig, though."

"Yeah. And who'd 'a thought that our little escapade would seem so insignificant when Nine Eleven came so close behind it?"

"Maybe so, but, if we hadn't succeeded, the New York and D.C. disasters would have been preceded with a nuclear holocaust in Seattle by only a few days. What a combination that would have made."

"The start of World War Three, do you think?"

"Anyhow, thanks, Mac," continued Peter, taking his hand.

"Lasso Lasso! For what," asked the cop. "Getting you involved in the whole mess from the beginning?"

Peter smiled and nodded towards the bride as she approached.

"Let's you and I get out of here and leave our guests to enjoy the party so they can trash the place," she laughed.

The crowd all came down to the water's edge to see them off. Jone jumped aboard to fire up the motors, and then he and Ramesh got the lines ready on the dock and prepared to cast off.

The newlyweds were headed on their honeymoon to Vatulele Island Resort. It was an exotic setting that would provide a great sendoff for their future together.

When they reached the cut at the hotel, they were greeted by an armada of boats all honking sirens and horns.

Slowly the *Noqui Tau* made her way through, to be accompanied till they reached open water in Beqa Lagoon, and then they were free.

Check out these other fine titles by
Durban House at your local book store.

EXCEPTIONAL BOOKS
BY
EXCEPTIONAL WRITERS

Current Titles

Nonfiction

FISH HEADS, RICE, RICE WINE & WAR: A VIETNAM PARADOX

   Lt. Col. Thomas G. Smith, Ret.

MIDDLE ESSENCE—WOMEN OF WONDER YEARS   Landy Reed

WHITE WITCHDOCTOR   Dr. John A. Hunt

PROTOCOL   Mary Jane McCaffree, Pauline Innis & Katherine Daley Sand

   For 25 years, the bible for public relations firms, corporations, embassies, governments and individuals seeking to do business with the Federal government.